Tipping the Balance

Poppy Green

DEDICATION

To the light and darkness that has moved me in friends, family and
strangers.

CONTENTS

ACKNOWLEDGMENTS

Extending love and gratitude to the ever discerning eye of my mum, who has supported my writing unconditionally. Thanks also to Ruth for her shrewd critiques and brutal honesty, and to Sarah for her unwavering curiosity in the progress of my work. Finally, thanks to my dad and Nigel Code for creating and producing the cover.

HOME TRUTHS

Nine o'clock in the morning. Priscilla Valentine hobbled determinedly towards her bedroom window, ready to catch Mr Heggarty undertaking his daily washing ritual. Drawing back her faded rose curtains, she saw with complacent satisfaction that he was half way through the delicate procedure. 'What a poor, strange man', she thought to herself, as she did every morning, watching the painstaking effort he put into hanging his whites in order of size, from smallest to largest. 'And the funniest thing is, he does it to impress me!', she marvelled, laughing out loud. 'Pity he's not my type, really', she lamented, eyeing his tatty grey cardigan with a haughty disdain, for there was no denying it was a lonely existence without her Kit, who had been gone eight years now.

Sitting in front of her gilt vintage dressing table, Mrs Valentine squinted hard at her reflection. 'Yes', she thought, pleased with herself. 'Ryan Hunter-Smith is right – you're still a dish at eighty.' For although her silver hair had lost the volume it once had, it still brought out her pale blue eyes a treat. 'Don't be jealous, Kit', she said, glancing devotedly at a photo of the young, handsome Mr Valentine who seemed to be eyeing her possessively from the corner of the mirror. 'No man could replace you, my dear!' What a wonderful man her Kit had been – so serious and talented. He had just finished his service in the Second World War when they met and had the air of a tortured soldier about him; skeletal and forlorn, he would often visit her parents' hardware shop for bike tools, and, she later discovered, to assess her potential as wife material. Young, blonde and pretty, she had been just his type, and he had taken her glamorous mother as an indication that she would age well. 'You certainly score top marks for thorough research!' she would later tell him, adoringly.

Unlike that despicable Joy Sullivan across the road, Mrs Valentine knew she was still alluring to the opposite sex. Good heavens, she had produced eight babies in her lifetime – eight! And so she got quite angry – although she never showed it - when Mrs Sullivan would come round bragging about the reams of supposed admirers she had. She would never forget the time Mrs Sullivan had sauntered into the local pub on the evening of Peter McCormack's birthday sporting a low-cut, navy blue taffeta dress, her ample bosom bursting out of the undersized garment like two potato sacks.

'Oh and that pathetic gold feather in her hair!', she remembered out loud. She really could have died with embarrassment for her poor friend. And to think she saw herself as having the pick of the crop that night, never mind her poor husband being present in the room. 'A greedy trollop, I'm sure!', she exclaimed.

Mrs Valentine often awoke at night convinced she could hear screaming babies. 'My babes!', she would cry, sitting bolt upright and solitary in her bed. So ingrained in her consciousness were the thirty years she spent child rearing that they had begun to seep with increasing lucidity into her present day reality. 'Oh what joyful days they were', she would chirp blithely to anyone who would listen. 'And then there were the soirées! So many successful people – artists, actresses and actors - under one roof, and all so elegantly turned-out! It really made one feel quite important.' And as she reminisced over her glory days, it was often said she appeared spellbound, her eyes distant with nostalgia, so listeners would feel apprehensive about breaking the spell and interrupting her flow, fearing her dejection as she hurtled back to reality with a bewildered thud.

Stepping cautiously down her winding staircase, Mrs Valentine absorbed the grandeur that emanated from Robin's family portrait, hanging high on the landing wall. 'What a sterling life he's carved for himself', she thought proudly, confronted with the three angelic faces of her grown up grandchildren, and Robin's beautiful slender wife smiling at him in awe. She had always known he would take after his father, for he had been an ambitious child, always top of the class and never without a pretty girlfriend. It had seemed inevitable that he would end up with a lucrative job that took him around the world, an exotic wife and holiday homes scattered across Europe. It was a pity, of course, that she hadn't seen him for three years but success breeds its own demands and she always got a birthday card from him and the family. 'How lovely that they still manage to remember my birthday with such busy lives', she would tell her friends. For there was no denying that Robin was her favourite. The others were wonderful too, of course, and some of them had done well for themselves, but not in the same way as her eldest.

Hobbling into the kitchen, the sight of her two finest bone china cups laid out on the side triggered the memory of a visitor she was expecting that morning. 'Ah yes, Peggy Underhill's to arrive at ten. Thank goodness for my coffee cups!', cried Mrs Valentine, feeling suddenly uplifted at the prospect of company. 'Oh but what to wear! God bless Mrs Underhill but she does have the habit of scrutinizing one with those eagle eyes of hers. All those years designing theatre costumes has made her quite fastidious', she muttered. And just as she began to mount the stairs again, the phone rang. 'Blast!', she exclaimed, hobbling over to the phone at the end of the dusky hallway.

'Bowdell 880351, speaking?', she announced in her ceremonious telephone voice. 'Ah Colin... yes?...I've not had time - Peggy Underhill's popping round for coffee and I'm still in my bedclothes, would you believe!...What?...Don't be silly, Colin – of course she's not! Oh you do confound me sometimes – honestly. Anyway, I really must go now as I've not even decided on an outfit to wear yet...Okay...See you shortly then.'

Shaking her head in exasperation, Mrs Valentine attempted another beeline for the stairs. 'Trust Colin to ring at such an inconvenient time *and* to contradict me again', she thought. It seemed to her that he made it his job to continually challenge her judgement and, besides that, he dressed shoddily, fooling himself into believing that being a painter and decorator gave him license to wear a messy ponytail and grubby overalls at all times.

Lately Colin had started bringing her cooked dinners, concerned she wasn't eating properly. He would call her every day without fail, usually at a time she deemed most inconvenient, and quiz her on what she had eaten that day. She would insist, and it was true, that her cupboards were full of the finest Waitrose produce, which had built up from the quarterly visits Richard, her middle child, would pay her. 'What a darling to drive all the way from London, the busy lawyer that he is, and shower me with bags full of my favourite cakes and delicacies. As if he doesn't have enough to tend to, I'm sure!', she would rattle off, digressing. Colin, however, would often appear to her at a loss for things to occupy him, taking time off work willy-nilly. 'It's a sorry state of affairs when a grown man has nothing better to do with his time than pester his poor mother over her eating habits', she imagined herself lamenting to Mrs Underhill. 'It was a terrible blow for his wife to leave with their daughter but I can quite see why she did it', she would continue. 'There are no prospects for an ageing painter and decorator, and she was such a glamorous woman'.

Dressing herself carefully in her favourite skirt and blouse, Mrs Valentine's mind wandered back to the many occasions in which she had perfected her hair and make-up, only for Kit to pounce on her with his characteristic carnal avarice, destroying hours of intricate adornment in one fell swoop. But she had been flattered by his unadulterated displays of lust, which he believed transcended practical matters of birth control. 'Good heavens, I don't have time for French letters!', he would exclaim should she ever volunteer the idea, since the babies were coming thick and fast. 'But I was lucky to have had a man who so loved and desired me', she would readily declare to anyone who questioned Kit's attitude to contraception.

Admiring herself in the full length mirror of her wardrobe, make-up and hair done to perfection, she felt convinced that Mrs Underhill could not find fault with her attire. And with that thought, she heard a knock at the door. Pushing open her bedroom window, she called down to Mrs Underhill to let herself in through the back gate. 'I'll be down shortly, my dear!' she cried. 'How lovely of her to travel all the way from Herefordshire to visit an old friend', she thought. 'It'll be like old times, gossiping over coffee and cake while the children were at school. Heaven forbid that Colin should turn up in his dirty overalls and make a mockery of himself, and me in the process!'

On reaching the kitchen, she threw open the hatchway into the front room, instructing Mrs Underhill to make herself at home. 'It pains me to say it, Peggy, but I've had to start taking precautions with my valuables lately. Colin's started popping round to cook for me and this seems to have coincided with the disappearance of some of my most cherished items. The beautiful silver vase that Kit's parents bought us as part of our wedding present is the latest in a row of objects to disappear – terrible really. To think one's son is capable of stealing from his own mother!

Mrs Underhill had not aged a jot - that Mrs Valentine was sure of. 'You are quite the same as I remember you in our prime, my dear!

How wonderful that you've kept so well over the years.' Mrs Underhill eyed her friend keenly and sympathetically, conveying an expression of recognition at her turquoise ensemble. 'Oh Priscilla, I wish I could say the same for you my dear. But I see that eight children and a miserable husband have finally taken their toll on you. I always feared they would get the better of you one day and it seems I was right to have thought so.'

Mrs Valentine could have died on the spot, and almost felt she should just to spite her so-called friend. 'This can't be happening to me', she told herself, her heart leaping into her mouth so she felt she would choke on it. 'Nothing beats a supportive husband and a minimal child quota for preserving one's youthful looks', continued Mrs Underhill, 'And here's a home truth, Priscilla – you didn't fare well in either department! My Jim was a fine husband and we spent many a happy year together. But tell me – did Mr Valentine ever cheer up?' Despite finding herself temporarily speechless, Mrs Valentine somehow mustered the words to defend her deceased husband. 'Oh he was a lovely man, really. Stern and taciturn, but he'd witnessed some blood curdling sights in the war. What's more, he fathered eight precious children, *most* of whom have gone on to lead rich and rewarding lives', she fought back, guarded and breathless.

Desperately seeking to steer the conversation away from her marriage, Mrs Valentine attempted to divert her friend's attention with news of her recent contact with an old heartthrob who had worked alongside their husbands in television. 'Anyhow, you might be interested to know that Ryan Hunter-Smith has been phoning me of late, proposing that he take me out – after all these years, can you believe!' 'But Priscilla, darling,' Mrs Underhill remarked drily. 'It seems you are in store for another home truth - Ryan Hunter-Smith is dead!'

Suddenly Mrs Valentine awoke in her armchair to a loud knocking sound. 'Who is it?', she chirped forcedly. 'It's Colin, Mum', came her son's concerned voice from outside. 'Are you going to let me in?' Rising stiffly from her chair, she hobbled to the door and unbolted it. 'You've come at a rather inconvenient time again, Colin', she announced. 'Mrs Underhill's here. She must've popped to the toilet, but she just told me some sad news – Ryan Hunter-Smith is dead.' Looking anxiously at his mother, Colin made his way into the kitchen to prepare her lunch. Just as he anticipated, there was no sign she had eaten breakfast, the counter remaining as pristine as her cleaner had left it the evening before. Opening the fridge, he found her treasured silver engagement vase sandwiched between two milk bottles.

'That's funny', remarked a despondent sounding Mrs Valentine. 'Mrs Underhill seems to have disappeared...'

Colin placed the silver vase carefully on his mother's kitchen windowsill and put the kettle on.

Of course she had laid her own trap by telling him she could relate to polyamory. What paradoxical creatures we are, saying one thing but needing something altogether different. In that moment, though, she had meant it; they were strangers and she had been carefree.

A few hours later, Lucy Young was standing naked in the bath, her right leg propped up on the side so as to allow Romain easier access to the condom that had disappeared deep inside of her. A light brown trickle of blood ran down the edge of the white porcelain; the tail end of her period, at least. There was nothing she could do but laugh incredulously.

'I thought this only happened in French films', she said, attempting to detach herself from the general discomfort and stark – albeit necessary – invasion of privacy she was experiencing.

'Welcome to Paris!', Romain replied, seconds before locating the soiled condom, wrapping it efficiently in tissue and flushing it away.

'The city of visceral dreams', she retorted in a post-coital daze, wrapping herself in a towel and drifting back towards his bed. But this was actually real.

Lying there, sobered by the physical invasion she had just encountered, she felt an urge to justify her impulsiveness.

'In case you were wondering, this was not my intention', she said.

'Mine neither', Romain replied, eying her quizzically.

'Women always seem driven to analyse situations they find themselves in', he continued in his thick French accent. 'Life is for living, not for picking apart'.

'Maybe because women tend to be more complex', she retorted, suddenly perturbed that she was lying naked next to someone who would struggle to understand the conflicting workings of her mind.

'My needs are just as complex as any woman's. I have a girlfriend but that won't stop me from meeting my destiny.'

'And it doesn't concern you that her destiny is already intertwined with yours?'

He rolled onto his side impulsively so that their eyes were level and examined her face with a sardonic grin. 'Yours could be too'.

'Not likely!', she cried. 'As if I'd invite such a shitstorm into my life?' She had a talent for fooling herself and others with assertive statements like these.

'We'll see', he grinned, running his fingers artfully along her receptive body.

It had been a liberating sensation finding herself alone at the airport that morning, responsible only for herself and 30 kilograms of luggage. The preceding months had bred a mixture of fear and anticipation in her. Aware that it was time to attempt a new life for herself, she'd still been plagued with the usual anxieties that accompany fresh starts. But the resolve of purpose she experienced as she hauled her cases across the seemingly endless expanse of glistening white tiles, their luminosity enhanced by the glaring rays of the midday sun, had felt like an awakening. Despite the physical encumbrance of her luggage, she became conscious of a lightness of being; a release from the psychological restraints that an over familiarity with people and places can induce.

A sense of possibility and renewal hummed in the air and flickered in the eyes of passing strangers as she made her way to meet Romain. The unfamiliarity of her surroundings evoked a liminal space in which potential lurked round every corner like the crest of a wave. Recalling the small, stagnant hole her London life had become, she reflected on the stifling intimacy of her friendships, the insidious, incurable disease that was slowly killing her father. For although she had remained free from the major commitments and responsibilities of adulthood, more often than not she'd still felt trapped. Waiting for Romain at a café on the corner of a bustling street, her 30kg of possessions at her feet, she had felt instinctively that she must preserve this lightness of spirit.

Suddenly he was walking towards her. She knew instantly that it was Romain, his expression and stride displaying recognition and purpose.

'You're late', he declared, abrupt and ruffled but still kissing her on both cheeks. He looked different to his photograph; pallid with an unfavourably large nose, but his eyes held the same intensity.

'Sorry – my phone only just got signal so I wasn't able to contact you before – have I held you up for something?'

'I was waiting for 3 hours - you said you were arriving at midday. There is some furniture I need to pick up from a shop near my place. We will go now or it will close'.

Had she not been so intoxicated by novelty, she might have taken Romain's brusqueness more personally. As it was, she perceived him and his contrariness with a curious sense of detachment.

'When I said midday I meant that's when I'd be arriving at the airport – I should've been more specific though – sorry', she said as they headed to his car. He left her struggling with her luggage for the first lap of their walk - an obvious punishment she had thought, amused – before offering to help her after she stopped to catch her breath in the middle of the street.

'It's a lot of stuff you bring for a holiday?', he enquired, eying her inquisitively.

'I've not come here for a holiday – I've come here to live! James didn't mention that?'

'To *live*?'

'Yes…'

'Why Paris?'

'It was the first city I ever felt really at home in, I guess – there's something refined and magical about it; it's exotic without being too foreign.'

He glanced at her then as if he were seeing her for the first time. 'And you don't know anyone here?'

'Correct'.

'Who did you come with on your first visit?'

'An ex- boyfriend of mine – we came here together a couple of times actually'.

Another penetrating gaze as he held open the door to an underground car park they had reached. He was definitely thawing. More than thawing, even. There was something predatory in that look. Don't buy into it, she told herself, recalling the airport's glistening white tiles. She must endeavour to keep this slate clean - he was just another face in the crowd.

'So what brought you to London last year?', she enquired, as they sped along endless Parisian boulevards, smouldering in the afternoon sun.

'I was supposed to meet a girl there', he began, hesitating for a moment,' but she cancelled on me at the last minute so I had to find some cheap accommodation', he concluded, glancing at her intermittently as if to gauge her reaction. A humble womaniser, at least, she thought, resisting his glances in favour of the wide open streets and faceless crowds.

'I found James on a sofa surfing website, he put me up for a few nights and now I return him the favour by hosting you!'

'It's really good of you - great how one connection can lead to another', she replied, instantly regretting her use of the word 'connection' and its implied depth. He smiled, raising his eyebrows suggestively, as if he had construed her comment in exactly the way she hoped he wouldn't.

It was a relief to get out of the stifling heat of Romain's car and stretch her legs in the dishevelled hardware shop at which they finally arrived. Rooting absent-mindedly through a box of musty books, she realised how encroaching his presence had been; it was as if the urgency of his temperament combined with the oppressive heat of the sun had created a microcosmic universe within those four metallic walls. Looking up, she caught him watching her from where he was queuing at the counter and was gripped by an unwelcome sense of gratification at his apparent desire for her. She shuddered at the thought that his gaze could already be possessing her.

'Just let me know if you need any help', she said, gravitating towards him in the queue.

'Maybe you could help me lift that chest of drawers into my car?' he replied, pointing to a shoddy contraption plied carelessly with black varnish. As they heaved the chest of drawers towards the car, she was struck by the elemental forces of masculine and feminine at play between them, her thin arms shaking uncontrollably under the strain, inept at the business of lifting in contrast to his innate robustness.

Physical strength and testosterone were not qualities that had appealed to her before but she was suddenly experiencing a powerful biological attraction; the lure of survival, perhaps. His body seemed just as capable of possession as his eyes and the pungent odour of his sweat hinted at a powerful virility. Nature will take its course, she resolved as he lodged the furniture securely into the car boot, accepting the futility of resistance to primal instincts. The act of sex can still be faceless, she told herself.

A man came over to the car to charge them for the chest of drawers and she felt suddenly obliged to return Romain's favour as he had returned James's.

'I'll pay half', she insisted. 'Call it penance for being late'.

'If you're sure?', he said, displaying no obvious resistance to her offer. 'I'm always short of money – Paris will rob you of every cent you have.'

'Absolutely', she replied, handing over 20 euros with apparent insouciance but inwardly struggling with the notion of co-dependency; so reassuring on one level but so diminishing on another. Bizarre how they'd not even known each other for twenty-four hours but were already buying furniture together, she thought, taking her place in the passenger seat.

Back at his top floor apartment, Lucy stood at the kitchen window admiring the vast expanse of rooftops stretching out before her, a sea of unknown destinies. She felt the sense of opportunity that came with new horizons, and was excited by the concept of herself as an inscrutable foreigner. Seconds later, Romain was standing in front of her, deliberate and monopolizing, his physical form eclipsing the intricate landscape her mind's eye had been contemplating.

'Honey vodka?', he offered, handing her a glass.

'Pourquoi pas', she joked, taking the drink and manoeuvring past his body towards the space of the front room. She couldn't decide whether she found his physicality encroaching or enticing now. Seating himself a little closer to her than she would have liked, a frustration suddenly rose in her.

'Do you always use alcoholic nectar to seduce your women?' she heard herself say.

'Not always', he replied, winking at her.

The vodka soon swayed their discussion towards matters of the heart.

'I'm under no illusions about love', Lucy said as they discussed previous relationships.

'Monogamy and happiness don't seem to be linked. Maybe polyamory is the way forward – at least we would stay liberated that way.'

She was playing her usual game of reverse psychology now, taking advantage of her outsider status and defying her instinct to be loved wholly and exclusively, providing there was room to breathe and be. He looked at her as though she had just answered his prayers and in that moment she felt he could gladly possess her.

'I think we should embrace the universal chaos – collapse into a million stars', he replied, leaning in to kiss her.

So she was his star of the moment, she deduced, kissing him back in a mood of fatalistic abandon.

'But there is a universe in every star', she said forcedly between kisses. She always hoped that men might penetrate her bravado, challenge her contrariness.

'Anything that brings us closer to cosmic consciousness is good for me', he continued, pulling off her dress with a Latino urgency that bore contempt for such obstacles to raw passion. The lightness she had experienced earlier was now being supplanted by the weight of Romain's sturdy physique on top of her, kissing her insatiably as though impassioned by his small step towards enlightenment. Aware she was supporting his egocentric dream, she acknowledged her defeat in the face of the delicious relief that accompanied physical possession in an unfamiliar city.

'And free love in the city of love is good for me', she replied, the glistening white tiles of that morning already accumulating the murky stains of time.

After all, she told herself - I'll be gone tomorrow.

MYOPIA

He had always felt more at ease in chaotic environments. It was their inherent promise that anything was possible, that reality was just a mirage, which reassured him.

'That's it, Mary, if you could just look up to the ceiling for me one more time then we'll be done', he declared, feebly attempting an authoritative voice.

'Robots robots robots – the lot of ya's!', she spat, her bloodshot eyes dancing with indignation. 'How's about I just pluck them out and pop them on a plate?', she continued in her drawling Yorkshire accent.

Guy knew that his professional façade was a futile strategy when dealing with the demented but he was still in the habit of testing the sight of sane people; people with an awareness, at least, of the protocol required on a trip to the optician's. It had occurred to him recently that his hands no longer shook whilst testing the eyes of his new patients; a clientele beyond discerning such tell-tale signs of malaise had obviously worked in his favour.

'But I thought you were waiting to go home, Mary? All you need to do is look up to the ceiling for me one more time and then you're free to go and pack your bags.'

Some might say using emotional blackmail on a mentally ill old woman was unscrupulous, but in this case he felt justified; Mary's reality wasn't related to external events. All she had was her inner world, its content unfolding in spurts of whimsical claptrap.

'It's you who needs your eyes testing if you think I'm that much of a pushover!', she snapped, scanning his face with a sardonic grin reminiscent of his old headmistress. 'Mummy's coming for me tomorrow so you'll have to do better than that.'

And in a gesture of begrudging consent, Mary looked up to the ceiling, enabling him to complete her test. His ploy had worked. Mummy, to whom Guy was indebted, had conveniently reminded her of the necessity of such check-ups. Mary had been a difficult patient but he enjoyed her defiance and conviction that she, and perhaps Mummy too, were the only sane people remaining on a planet full of lunatics. Maybe they were, he thought, as he saw her out to the lounge and informed the manager for the umpteenth time that day that 'she needs new'.

Guy found locum work with the new agency a breath of fresh air after the oppressive working environment at Vision Plus. Although it had taken losing his job through a humiliating drugs bust, resulting in him pleading guilty to seven charges of drugs possession, receiving a twelve month conditional discharge and being midway through a succession of court hearings, his life had opened up monumentally. The flexibility of moving from one home to another was a revelation to him, as were the nebulous mental landscapes of his patients; he saw them as an antidote to his former boss, Michelle, known amongst friends as the Bitch in The Power Suit. Everything about her, from her streamlined pinstriped suit with the strikingly large shoulder-pads, to her painstakingly fixed top-knot and immaculately made up poker face, had suggested to him an extreme distaste for fallibility. He recalled their first encounter and how, no doubt impressed with his first class degree in Optical Science, she seemed to have been anticipating someone with similar levels of consistency in confidence and identity.

'Guy Matthews?', she'd enquired a little too ecstatically, an obvious attempt to conceal her bewilderment at the anxious, pony-tailed apparition standing outside her office.

'Yes!', he'd replied, mirroring her parody of upbeat assertiveness. Then there was the confused expression on her face; the troubled squint as she caught sight of his trembling hands.

'Wonderful!', she'd exclaimed, ushering him into her office, at which point Guy concluded she was the type who tended to say the opposite of what they actually thought. 'Let's get down to business, then!', she'd continued, still measuring him up while sustaining what he imagined must be an excruciating smile.

Michelle had incited in him the combined sentiments of terror and rebellion. Her formidable brand of dominatrix authority was the sort he had always harboured an ironical respect for. But the realisation he would be working long hours in close proximity to her had filled him with dread. He had quickly sensed she would not miss a thing, her darting eyes reminiscent of his old physics tutor's at college. Although Mr Blundell had never humiliated him, the old man had often displayed penetrating insights into other pupils' shortcomings. Guy recalled the terrifying moments in which his hesitations had tested Blundell's patience, the latter seeming to uncover a new vulnerability in him with every passing second. He was convinced that this man had clocked his homosexuality and was waiting for an

18

opportune moment to make some facetious reference to it. Although this never actually happened, he was sure his fear-induced hyper-attentiveness during these classes was the main reason he'd graduated with an A in physics.

Waiting outside the room of his next patient, he saw Mary and her Zimmer frame pushing purposefully towards him.

'Mummy…mummy…is that you?', she croaked, her musty voice alive with hope.

'No, Mary, it's Guy – remember me! - I just tested your eyes.' He was tempted to masquerade as Mummy both for her benefit and out of sheer curiosity but the manager was in close proximity and had made clear to him the distinction between the residents' raving lunacy and the staff's unwavering sanity.

'My my', she remarked, squinting at him with eager curiosity. 'You are a pretty boy aren't you? All the soft features of a woman. Not to worry though, love. I'm sure you're every inch a real man!'

'Thanks, Mary. You can be quite charming when you want to be!', Guy replied, strangely flattered.

She might be blind as a bat but she's onto something, he thought. It was only last week he'd featured as a transvestite in one of the more upmarket women's magazines – a spontaneous, devil-may-care reaction to leaving Vision Plus. His old friend Rachel had coaxed him into it on a whim, eager to parody the trashy sensationalism that dominated the women's magazine market and earn some cash in the process. A few months on, he and another 'Bearded Laydee' were splurged across the front cover of Hunny magazine, resplendent in spandex leggings, towering bouffants and red lipstick, a 'Real Life' caption sporting the headline, 'My Man Left me for a Bearded Laydee'. He had been a little ruffled when the story materialised, having not believed it actually would, but reassured that his world view had been vindicated; it was all a raving farce.

It was a mad world. This was one of the few things Guy was sure of. He had just received a pay rise and was now earning around 350 pounds a day prescribing glasses to the clinically insane who would thus be better equipped to stare vacantly at Jeremy Kyle on repeat all day. Despite his acknowledgement that for most of the residents, seeing was no longer believing, he was reassured to find that many of them were living out their own rose-tinted fantasies, glasses or no glasses. Ethel, Guy acknowledged, was one of the aforementioned.

'Where's my kiss then?' the scarecrow woman, who glided towards him, asked.

She was, according to her notes, 91 years old. The fat care worker trailing behind her looked as if she could do with some of her patient's vitality, Guy noted, greeting her with a polite nod. Then he remembered that he was probably earning ten times what she was and offered her a guilty smile as she led them to a room at the end of the corridor.

'That's some dress, Ethel!', he remarked, entranced by the psychedelic floral vision before him. She had even managed to co-ordinate her nails and lipstick and seemed blissfully unaware of the long string of dribble that dangled threateningly from her chin to her breast.

'I'd say that outfit warrants a kiss', he continued, not that this affirmation made any difference to Ethel, who was apparently hell bent on getting her way. Seconds later her bright pink lips were planted firmly on his clean shaven cheek, the string of dribble uniting with his freshly laundered shirt. *C'est la vie*, he thought, surrendering to the futility of keeping up appearances in the face of the slobbering woman that embraced him.

'OK Ethel, if you could just sit down and look up to the ceiling for me…', he began, his cheek smeared with lipstick, a dubious looking wet patch crowning the right breast pocket of his shirt. A satisfied looking Ethel looked up for him obediently and he felt as he examined her hard worn retina that they were two of a kind. Not only did he covet her dress but he perceived the perverse sense of joy she derived from smearing his cheek with lipstick. He imagined it was similar to the sensation he'd first experienced seeing himself sprawled across a woman's magazine in drag. Perhaps even reminiscent of the surge of pleasure he'd encountered after his scandalous behaviour at the Eye Ball.

'You got pink paint on your face now, Sir!', Ethel blurted in her strong Devonshire accent as Guy wrote out her prescription. He knew it would be just a matter of time before she vented her delicious secret, her wiry body tense with suppressed anticipation.

'I hope you're joking, Ethel? I can't have my patients thinking I'm a clown!', he replied, obeying the rules of the game. This was enough to propel her into a fit of unshakeable hysterics for several minutes and put him officially behind schedule. But if he could provide such unadulterated joy to an old dear on borrowed time then to hell with the schedule. There was no tyrant in a power suit breathing down his neck now; no expectations for him to be the detached, punctual authority figure. He wrote out Ethel's prescription in a leisurely fashion, serenaded by her infectious laughter.

Forewarned by the fat care worker that David, his next patient, had a bark that was worse than his bite, Guy was unsure whether to be reassured or disturbed, but decided he was above all grateful for the abnormality of his clients. At Vision Express, he had been the freak. An average day there would begin with a jeering remark from Michelle - 'What did they put in your coffee this morning?' being a favourite – which only served to increase his shakes and prompt baffled expressions from his patients. 'He'll have my eye out in a minute', he'd hear them thinking as he did his best to pass the time with a few polite questions. Fortunately, all examined eyes remained intact, despite Michelle's tyrannical presence and his ever increasing existential woes.

As he approached the room of his next patient and heard the macabre exclamation, 'help me, I'm dying!', he breathed a sigh of relief at no longer having to keep up appearances; all freaks together here, he muttered quietly to himself .

David was his most physically disturbing patient so far. Suspended in a ceiling hoist, his body inclined in a foetal position, dark eyes staring at Guy from the bearded confines of a grey, skeletal face, he proceeded mechanically with his morbid chant, 'help me, I'm dying, help me I'm dying!' Guy considered the euphemistically named Primrose Lodge, deciding House of Horrors would be a more fitting epithet for the home. That said, he found the primacy of this kind of horror reassuringly uncalculated.

'Don't take any shit from him', the care worker warned before leaving them. 'He used to be a headmaster and still thinks he rules the school, don't you Cowgell?', she continued, shooting him a haughty look before waddling off down the corridor. So that's how she got her kicks, Guy thought, approaching David Cowgell with renewed awe.

'Hello Mr Cowgell', he began apprehensively. 'I'm just here to test your eyes, okay?' The decrepit old man eyed him sternly, suspending his chant to concentrate, and a pregnant silence hung in the air. Guy observed a fierce intelligence in his eyes and imagined all the pupils he'd once terrified with this formidable stare.

'You've got pink paint on your face, boy!', Mr Cowgell bellowed in a pedagogical tone at odds with his shrivelled, emaciated physique, and Guy felt himself instantly transformed into a child again. 'And that shirt's seen better days, too', the old pedant added, his unrelenting eye scanning Guy from head to toe.

'You're right there', Guy replied, feeling defeated and superfluous alongside Mr Cowgell's apparently impeccable sight. 'This might sound like an excuse', he continued, 'but I've just finished with a patient who was keen to transform me into a laughing stock – her heart was in the right place though, so I didn't get too upset!'

'Always excuses with you people', the old man grunted as Guy set his equipment down on the bedside table. Let him have his glory, he thought, maintaining a submissive silence as he prepared the necessary selection of lenses and erected the vision testing drum at the foot of the bed. The silence appeared to send Mr Cowgell back into a morbid trance and after a minute or so his eyes had glazed over and he proceeded with his chant. Despite claiming to be dying, Guy thought the old man appeared more relaxed when involved in his lament, as if he were surrendering to all those years spent as an authority figure. He sensed he had his work cut out as he interrupted his patient with the spotlight for the Retinoscopy test.

'Sorry to hear you're in so much distress, Mr Cowgell, but if you wouldn't mind looking up to the ceiling for me…',Guy began, summoning him from his trance and encouraging a livid headmaster back to the room again.

'Come a step closer, boy, and you'll receive the punishment of a lifetime!', he threatened, his eyes fierce and uncompromising. Guy stopped still, sensing it was best to do as he was told, especially when he noticed Mr Cowgell's hand reaching menacingly down the back side of his trousers. 'I've done it before and I'll do it again, I don't doubt', he continued, and Guy was dismayed to learn that the old man meant business as he brazenly revealed a handful of ripe excrement, his eyes twinkling triumphantly. Inclining his head and making a beeline for the door, Guy wondered whether the fat care worker's warning had, in fact, been literal.

Deciding a tea break was necessary, he headed to the staff kitchen. It was the old man's abject defiance that Guy could relate to; his will to transgress. He suspected Mr Cowgell had long possessed a compulsion to behave in a manner that transcended expectation; a reflex, perhaps, stemming from his former position of authority and power. Guy thought it was a similar reflex in himself that had led to his current position at Primrose Lodge. He remembered his last morning at Vision Plus; walking into the office, bleary eyed and on edge after another night of reckless indulgence, anticipating Michelle's derisive comments, receiving them in due course alongside the news that he was now on a trial period, his sales having been 'below par'. His response had been metaphorically comparable to Mr Cowgell's; abject and desperate, with intent to soil the reputation of his boss and escape from his own misery. Lowering the tone, he had decided, would be his ticket to autonomy.

If Michelle was so obsessed with finding chinks in his already feeble armour, the Eye Ball had been a perfect occasion to reveal them; it had synchronised with his need to break the cycle of lies and repetition his life had become. An event of pomp and ceremony: champagne and canapés, polite conversation, keeping up appearances despite increasing levels of intoxication, and it had fallen on the evening of the day he'd been put on trial. Of course there was going to be a scene, he reflected with hindsight.

He recalled Michelle's prolonged glance as he greeted her and the party at the hotel lobby that evening. She'd sensed his fearlessness, he was sure. He'd arrived at the event prepared: a stash of white powder and a slinky black dress folded neatly in a carrier bag; essential tools to bridge the gap between his two disparate existences. Knowing he was soon to break free from the oppressive world of Vision Plus had endowed him with a sense of liberty he'd not experienced for some time. So much so, it seemed, that Michelle had avoided eye contact with him although they were sitting practically opposite one another. Guy had noticed that despite her particularly sleek power suit and impenetrable makeup, her hold over him had suddenly diminished. 'It's an especially sophisticated suit you're sporting tonight, Michelle', he'd found himself shouting to get her attention. She glanced at him dubiously, washing back a sizable gulp of champagne. 'Wish I knew your secret! You always look so...what's the word? Impervious?' She took another hasty gulp of her drink before attempting to steer his attention away from her spurious perfection. 'Oh Guy, it's kind of you to say but these things are so easily said after a fist-full', she spat softly back at him. 'Ah but in wine there is truth – isn't that what they say?', he retorted effortlessly. Michelle's expression now resided somewhere between curiosity and terror.

'Of course, Guy', she replied drily, rising from her chair in a gesture of resignation. 'I'm flattered by your genuine fascination with my wardrobe – you're the only man I've ever known to demonstrate such an interest in it', she concluded, winking at him before grinning conspiringly at the nearby company and heading to the toilets.

So she'd sussed his penchant for women's clothing; Guy could have sworn he'd been nothing but discreet about his fetish. Why waste any more time in his male attire then, he'd thought, knocking back his glass of champagne and seizing the moment to head to the toilets and slip into a dress. Sniffing the remains of his white powder, he was resolved that it would be his last dalliance with the stuff in view of his imminent liberation. It wasn't long before he was soaring high into the cosmos, weightless and invincible, as if Icarus's wings had sprouted from his dress, setting him up for the sweetest of declines.

From this point on, his memory of the night consisted of hazy snippets of dialogue and slapstick encounters that could have been taken from a comedy of errors: grabbing Michelle by the arms and spinning her around the room to eighties rock, insisting he could never compete with her immaculate persona – 'It must get tiring, forever ensuring everything's in its place' –, pelvic thrusting an attractive male colleague and re-gaining consciousness outside the hotel in the early hours of the morning, aware of the potent stench of what he presumed to be his own vomit on the steps beside him and the menacing sound of approaching police sirens.

Despite his double vision, Guy had been able to distinguish Michelle's apparition on the nearby roadside. Squinting harder, he deciphered two policemen guiding her handcuffed silhouette towards him. Michelle in handcuffs? No doubt indulging some S&M fantasy, he'd told his inebriated self, until the reality of the situation became clear.

'Don't worry, Guy - you're not hallucinating. We've probably got more in common than either of us would care to admit', she remarked drily, and he noticed how her voice tailed off uncharacteristically at the end of this obscure statement.

'Guy Patterson?', intercepted the lumbering police man to Michelle's right. 'P.C Sowton of the Avon Police. Good night, was it?', he continued with a smirk on his face, clearly not inviting a response. Just as well since Guy found himself temporarily speechless. 'Do me a favour now and stand up so I can search you'.

Sprawled shamelessly across the concrete steps, his slinky black dress stained with vomit and riding unbecomingly between his legs, he rose unsteadily to his feet, and in a spontaneous gesture of defeat, reached into his pockets and handed the officer his remaining drugs stash. Bewildered and unable to verbally articulate himself, Guy's instinct had been to open his arms with loving surrender to his bemused onlookers but he was swiftly blocked as he went to embrace them.

'You can stop right there, sunshine. We're not here to get fruity with you. If you want to get frisky you'll be facing the music with a nice pair of handcuffs like your lovely colleague here. No exceptions just because you're both off your rockers.'

Meeting his boss's gaze, the truth stared brazenly back at him. She was, of course, just as much of an addict as he was. If he hadn't been so preoccupied with keeping his own head above water it would have been glaringly obvious from the start.

'I hope you can see why I dragged you down with me, Guy – I was the epitome of inconspicuous next to your outrageous behaviour and somehow I'm the number one criminal – utter insanity!'

Watching her layers of composure slowly unravelling, Guy felt strangely akin to the Bitch in the Power Suit, realising they'd both finally reached an equal footing.

'Only human I guess', was the sole response he could muster. It's all too surreal, he thought to himself, smiling at his crestfallen boss, unsure if he was ready to part with the superhuman image of her he'd supported.

'Two of a kind if you ask me', the smaller, quieter policeman piped up as they walked towards the police car.

Guy chortled in baffled agreement, while Michelle glared vengefully at the policeman. But there was, Guy was certain, a faint smile on her face before she turned away in an obligatory show of disgust.

***

The fat care worker slouched into the kitchen, eying him curiously. 'He scared you off then, did he?', she inquired, putting the kettle on. 'He has the same effect on the rest of us here too – don't worry…'

Guy could see she was enjoying the idea of his defeat at the hands of Mr Cowgell. 'Well it was a choice between staying and being pelted with shit or taking a quick exit - I hadn't realised you were talking literally earlier', he said, eying her quizzically.

'It was just a warning, that's all. I didn't want to say too much and frighten you off', she replied.

'Sensitively handled, I'll give you that!', he laughed. 'I suppose I had to find out for myself...'

Impressively discreet for someone so apparently simple, he thought.

'You must have seen some sights working here', he continued, as Marie voraciously attacked a packet of custard creams.

'Nothing shocks me anymore,' she said, eying him sincerely for a moment before bolting another biscuit and leaving. Guy saw she wasn't bluffing. He imagined her keeping her deadpan expression as he metamorphosed into a dress and stilettos on the spot, which immediately killed any lurking desire to do so. She wasn't looking for cracks and weak spots in others: she'd seen enough of those to last her a lifetime. They were a shameless bunch here; all guilty, all free.

PATTERNS

Carla received the phone call early that morning. She listened with measured intent as she heard the news she had resigned herself to expect. Glancing at the note Steve had left her on the kitchen table, she flinched with regret. "Popped out for a bit—won't be long." He knew, she lamented. Why else would he scoot off without explaining his plans?

Hanging up the receiver, she stopped still for a moment. The kids' breakfast bowls were   perched on the side, half filled with milk and a few floating cornflakes—one of Steve's pet hates. She poured the milk down the sink as if it were the beginning of a normal day. By the time she'd placed the bowls on the drainer, her instincts had flooded in. Grabbing the car keys, she dashed out into the morning haze.

The hospital was a seventeen mile drive from the family home. Carla usually savoured the journey along the still winding roads of Somerset countryside into the realm of civilization. Her job as a music teacher saw her travel to Tiverton—the closest town to her quiet hamlet—most days. She would relish those forty minutes of 'her' time, alone with her music and her thoughts, darting past the ever changing colours and forms of nature.

But today was different. The empty roads ahead seemed desolate and the dark trees that lined them were ominous. Uncertainty, it seemed, was all that lay ahead.

Richard's appearance at the house last Friday had forced her to address the questions which, for the past twenty years she had attempted to suppress. It was late afternoon and she had been indulging in some quiet time after a hectic day of teaching. As she lazed, half reading on the sofa, she discerned a sense of urgency in the motion of a figure walking up the garden path. Seconds later, some aggravated knocking occurred, followed by the swinging open of the front door.

He stood in the hallway, awkward yet purposeful. She noted a heavy jowl peppered with graying stubble and penetrating hazel eyes that were instantly identifiable, transporting her immediately back to her youth. A pregnant silence resided in the ensuing seconds, during which she discerned a weight to his presence. Gone was the carefree spirit she remembered and in its place was a man who struggled with life. For years he had haunted her dreams, alerting her to what could have been. Bewildered and unable to speak she froze in shock, tears distorting her vision as if to shield her from his gaze.

Unfazed by her emotional reaction, Richard eyed her searchingly whilst maintaining a respectable distance.

'I had to see you', he said. 'I've had a long time to think about our past and something's been playing on my mind'.

Feeling powerless and exposed, she removed herself from his gaze and turned towards the front room.

'It's been twenty years, Richard. A little warning wouldn't have gone amiss', Carla retorted, her back turned towards him. Although many years had passed since their last embrace, the acute familiarity of his presence seemed to defy any passing of time. He edged closer, touching her shoulder and apologizing again.

Seeking a sense of normality from the clock above her head, she was unnerved to see that Steve and the kids were due home at any moment. Seconds later, Edward, her eldest son, walked through the door. There was, she knew, no way to normalize the situation, no way of concealing her bloodshot eyes.

'Edward, this is Richard – an old friend of mine and your Dad's', she said, forging a tone of light hearted enthusiasm. Edward stood hesitantly in the hallway, looking at Carla with concerned curiosity.

'Pleased to meet you, Edward', Richard said, holding out his hand. Edward shook it perfunctorily, evidently unsettled by the situation he had stumbled upon and Carla noticed in Richard's expression a hint of vindication as he scrutinized her son.

Once Edward had excused himself, Richard took his cue to leave, as if his curiosity had been satisfied. He turned and walked towards the door. Looking back, he gazed at her with an intimacy that spoke of their youth.

'I got your address from Barny – an old friend of Steve's from Woolacombe, remember him? I…there was something I needed to know'.

She understood but remained silent, afraid to hear the candour of his thoughts.

He left hastily and apologetically, in a manner as peculiar to that of his arrival. But she knew that something monumental had just occurred, the ripples of which would be felt thereafter.

Aware that her driving had become synchronized with the turbulence of her thoughts, Carla sought some light relief in the crass jabbering of the local radio station. The kids would be shocked, she thought, momentarily diverted by this. Willing herself to distraction, she listened to the facetious DJ probing a newly wed man about his current state of marital bliss and, of course, his gorgeous wife. She promptly flicked the off switch, irked by the fatuous cliché of happily ever after marriages.

Steve's earthy sensibilities had captivated her for the first few years. They had met on a beach in north Devon in 1969 and the attraction had been instant and all consuming. She was busking with her guitar on the promenade and noticed a lean, wavy haired figure watching her from a distance. There was something staid and steadfast about his presence. He had said to her, following the intimacy of their first night together, that there was gravity in their connection and that he felt they had a future. Although she struggled to imagine his vision of the future, she fell for his passionate convictions and married him a year later.

Despite her love for Steve, she had felt stifled by him early on in their relationship. The way he eyed her with unwavering intensity, as though she was an absolute, was unnerving to her. At first, she had been drawn to his solidity; she had craved to be rescued from the empty space that surrounded her and he had strolled into her sights at precisely the right moment, direct and self-assured. But she had wondered, despite the sincerity of his intentions, whether the strength of his convictions would ultimately drive her away.

She had met Richard a few months into her relationship with Steve. It was midsummer and a group of them were getting high on Woolacombe beach. An unkempt figure with long black hair and ripped jeans had ambled towards them, prompting cheers of excitement. He had just returned from a six month stint in South America and carried an air of mystique about him. Carla felt his magnetism instantly - penetrating eyes attuned to the intensity of the moment, a lusty smile on his face, as he dived into the group without losing his singularity. She was sitting on Steve's lap, but Richard's freewheeling presence had made her self-conscious about this arrangement, prompting her to slide discreetly off Steve and onto the blanket.

Steve had offered to put Richard up for a while after his travels, by which time Carla was a full-time resident at the house. He would often disappear for days on spontaneous adventures, full of restless intensity that only served to enhance Carla's fascination with him. One morning, he told her of his quest to expand his consciousness. He had taken plant medicine in the Amazon and experienced a harmony with himself and his surroundings he'd never dreamed was possible. Although New Age thinking was alien to her, having had a conventional, working class upbringing, Carla sensed a raw passion in Richard's pursuit. There was, she felt, something impossibly idealistic about him; an unattainable essence she longed to touch.

One evening when Steve was visiting his sister, Richard offered to cook for Carla. Despite acknowledging the inherent intimacy of a two person dining experience, she was quick to accept his invitation. It was the first time they had spoken at length without being accompanied by Steve and she found herself enjoying the freedom they had to converse directly, even flirtatiously. The chemistry between them had made their union later that evening a lingering inevitability.

The next few months were interspersed with secret liaisons. Carla was enrolled on a part-time music degree, granting her generous amounts of free time and Steve was working full-time as a gardener. Richard was doing sporadic shifts at a local pub, enabling him and Carla to steal some time together most days. The sordidness of their encounters charged their love making with a sense of urgency. She knew she was living on a knife-edge but that was the thrill of it. When Richard told her he loved her she felt lost to her better self; her imagination ran wild with fantasies of their future together.

Returning to the house one evening after a weekend at her parents', she was struck by the empty space that surrounded her. Richard's possessions had gone and Steve sat rigidly on the sofa, arms crossed. He told her they had thrown a party on the Friday night and that Richard had got drunk and antagonistic towards some of the group. When they challenged him, he had become aggressive and begun to lash out. Steve said he had woken the following morning to find that Richard had gone, having disclosed nothing of his destination.

Carla stood by the door, unable to articulate a response. She had been feeling faint all day and couldn't bring herself to do anything other than sink to the carpet and sit, disorientated. Steve eyed her anxiously before walking over to her, picking her up and carrying her to the sofa where they sat and talked. She attempted to probe him dispassionately about the events of Friday night but he refused to oblige her, arguing that Richard's selfish behaviour did not warrant the time and energy of an explanation. His cold reasoning only succeeded in isolating her, reinforcing her longing for Richard.

The following day, she discovered she was pregnant.

Now, twenty years on, as she neared the hospital, Carla found herself obsessing over the phone conversation she'd had with Richard the previous morning. She'd not heard from him since his visit a week before and had begun to feel less tense. Answering the phone to a resonant tone that was unmistakably his, she had felt her body immediately tauten.

'I know I shouldn't be calling you', he began tentatively, 'It's just that the past week has been torture for me; seeing you and the life you've created for yourself – well…it's been a stark reminder of my own failures; what I could've had'.

'Please cut to the chase', Carla demanded, agitated by his insensitivity to her plight.

'Okay', he said. 'Meeting Edward last week confirmed what I've always suspected to be true: that he's my son.'

Following his announcement that he could not rest until this was verified, she hung up.

Although she was not surprised by Richard's declaration, hearing him utter it had struck her to the core. A possibility that for years had remained unquestioned had finally been plucked from the void and transformed into a conceivable reality. She had chosen from the offset not to consider the chance that Edward was Richard's. His abrupt exit from her life at that crucial time had undone any future they may have had together. Moreover, Steve's elation at the news he was to be a father had given her the strength to draw an invisible line under her fantasy of a life with Richard.

Edward was the first person she saw as she entered the hospital foyer. He was sitting on a bench facing the sliding doors with an envelope in his hands. She was surprised to see him, as she had insisted that he go to college that morning, promising she would let him know when she heard from Steve. He looked at her knowingly, maintaining his gaze as he stood up to pass her the letter.

'Richard gave it to me after college yesterday', he said. 'I wanted an explanation from Dad, so I showed it to him'.

Steve had read the letter silently, making no attempts to deny Richard's allegations. Instead, he had copied Richard's phone number, called him and arranged to meet him later that evening, promising Edward they would get to the bottom of things.

'When I woke up and realised Dad hadn't come home, I called Richard and demanded he tell me what had happened. He was drunk, mumbling something about Dad paying for his righteousness. So I located his address on the letter, jumped in the car and drove to Dulverton, where I found Dad on a back road, unconscious in his car'.

Looking at her with eyes eager to understand, Edward seemed to be asking a thousand questions. She found herself unable to say anything other than that Steve had, and always would, love him like a father and that was what mattered. Beneath his puzzled expression, Carla was relieved to detect in him a germ of philosophical acceptance as to what would be. Although he wouldn't stay, he reassured her in his cool, adolescent manner that these things could be worked through. Never before had she invested so much hope in the optimistic workings of a young mind.

As she walked along the sterile corridors to the Accident and Emergency ward, Carla deplored Richard's sudden impact on their lives, like a meteor crashing gratuitously on a nest of fragile bonds. Why, she wondered, had he waited for twenty years to ravage the established order she had worked so hard to create?

Entering the ward, she spotted Steve instantly. Attached to a drip, his right leg bandaged and hoisted up and his face swollen and bruised, he eyed her solicitously as she approached him.

'I thought Edward could be Richard's', he said, before she had a chance to speak.

'I suspected it all along. I guessed there was something going on between you back then and Richard confirmed my suspicions the weekend you visited your parents. The fight at the party was actually between us and culminated with me kicking Richard out and warning him to stay away from the house.'

Carla remained silent while Steve explained how he had met Richard the previous evening to discuss his letter to Edward.

'He was drunk and contentious from the start, maintaining that you had only stuck with me for the purpose of stability but that your love for each other had been fervent and true and had produced a child. I told him that I had and always would love Edward as my son, whatever the results of a biological test might prove, and moreover, that he was clearly not psychologically fit to be a dad.'

Steve had learned from Barny that Richard had recently been discharged from a mental health unit, having suffered for twelve years with what was said to have been a form of psychosis.

Carla felt Steve's admissions wash over her like a breaking wave, washing away the remnants of her delusional fantasies.

'I'd seen women fall prey to Richard's charms before, thinking they could drift ethereally into the sunset with him, blind to his self-aggrandizing, manipulative streak. I loved you too much to sit back and watch him fool you', he said.

'And what about your cunning efforts to conceal the truth from me? I'd call that manipulation', Carla retorted.

'I loved you and wanted to save you from an unsustainable future with Richard. Come on, Carla. We've lived a fruitful, stable life with the kids that you could never have had with Richard. We work well together; make a good team.'

Acknowledging that her secret fantasies of a more fulfilling life with Richard could never have come to fruition, Carla saw she had become a victim of her own illusion. While she had imagined him travelling the globe, unfettered and carefree, he had been confined to an institution. She recalled his brooding intensity, how his presence would flood a room, and her mind delved back to their first meeting at the beach. There had been a spirit of light-hearted playfulness amongst the group that afternoon as they lazed about in the sun.

Then Richard had appeared. There were cheers of excitement, she had thought. The atmosphere had become charged and focused on his imminent approach; charged, it now came to her, with trepidation, even fear.

Steve broke the reflective silence that had resided between them and, as if he had read her mind, said 'People were wary of him – he had a paranoid, unstable streak that would erupt out of the blue. I was suspicious of him – I always knew he was capable of this'.

She studied his bruised face, his eyes flashing with anxious sincerity, and was gripped by the memory of the first night she and Richard had slept together. Looking into her eyes, he had said afterwards, 'I saw you move away from Steve when we met at the beach – you'll regret that one day'. Baffled, she had asked him to elaborate, to which he replied, 'I have a nasty habit of getting under people's skin – you'll see'.

Rolling onto her back, staring at the woodchip ceiling, she had felt herself intoxicated by Richard's precarious spirit. Lost in the complex patterns above her, she understood then that life's ambiguities would be a dangerous source of fascination to her.

As her focus shifted back to Steve, steady and enduring, something like contentment flowed through her as she envisaged the years ahead. The sun shone through the window, illuminating the room's white-washed walls. This time though, the patterns were missing.

TIPPING THE BALANCE

Masud awoke suddenly, a feeling of unease about him. Peeling his eyes open to a squint, he was confronted with the stark, half-naked body of Tilly, sprawled out on her back, mouth open, black vest top hanging loosely about her torso, vagina on full incriminating display. Blotches of rusty brown blood soaked through the tawny under sheet that lay in a crumpled mass beneath her. Leaping out of bed before his mind had time to ruminate, Masud tiptoed as swiftly and lightly as possible to the couch downstairs. What in hell's name? Tilly, his discrete, graceful tenant of a year, semi-naked and presumably paralytic in his bed? Tilly - the reserved, self-contained yoga teacher, who got her kicks from fermented milks and daily saunas?

Lying shell-shocked on the living-room couch, he began to reassure himself with the hard facts:

1.   He'd woken up fully clothed.
2.   He'd only drunk three pints at the Red Lion last night – not enough for any memory lapses to occur.
3. Nothing sexual had happened, to the best of his knowledge.

But why the lack of knickers? Was she just blind drunk or had her hormones possessed her? He was no stranger to the ravages of the menstrual cycle, and had born the brunt of its tempests many a time with his ex-wife. It was how Tilly would react when she came to that terrified him most. Despite grappling with a compulsion to flee the house, he knew that all he could reasonably do was lie with a sense of doom on the sofa, and wait for the drama to unravel. The clock read 06:12. He resigned himself to a long wait…

A couple of fraught hours passed before he heard footsteps coming from his room, directly above him, lingering in the hallway, diverting for a long minute or two into her room, before making their way downstairs in an arrhythmic, hesitant trot. Taking a deep, apprehensive breath, Masud stood up and attempted to busy himself, pointlessly arranging newspapers on the coffee table into an orderly pile. He felt her presence in the doorway, heard her clearing her throat, at which point he turned to face her.

'Morning…so I've just woken up half-naked in your bed. What the…?' Apparently speechless, she let out a nervous, staccato laugh that fell abruptly flat, like a choked engine.

Dressed in tight black jeans and the same black vest top, her blonde hair pulled softly back from her face, fringe falling loosely to the side, Masud was surprised to see Tilly looking her elegant, fresh-faced self. It was only her mystified expression that gave her away. Sensing her bewilderment and discomfort as she stood awkwardly in the doorway, a soul in limbo, his fear of accusation dissolved into compassion for her. He decided some humour was called for:

'Well, I don't know, Tilly. If one thing's certain, though, it's that I'm gonna have to start locking my door at night!'

She laughed, a little more naturally this time, and their eyes met for a brief, tentative moment as he edged his way past her into the open space of the dining room.

'Probably a wise move', she replied, a hint of irony in her voice, as she trailed loosely behind him.

He began to busy himself with the process of coffee making, the dispersion of tension through practicalities being one of his gifts.

'Nothing happened between us, anyhow', he said, turning briefly to face her, intuiting that the elephant in the room should be addressed and conquered without further delay.

'I only had a few pints at the Lion last night', he continued, returning with concentrated precision to the spooning of coffee grains into the cafetiere.

'Not usually enough to suffer any memory loss.'

He was hoping she would take his unwillingness to pummel absolutes for sincerity rather than evasion of some sordid truth. *Life is full of grey areas,* was one of his mother's most hackneyed expressions, and he had undoubtedly been indoctrinated by it over the years, his preferred offshoot being the equally hackneyed, *Tell it like it is.* (And not *like you think you should,* he would forcibly add).

He turned once again to gauge her response, letting the hot tap run for a few moments before rinsing the coffee cups. She was staring abstractedly at the floor, but when she looked up to meet his gaze he was comforted by her relieved expression, as if she had just surfaced from a bad dream. Something in her bearing had softened and relaxed.

36

'Well that's reassuring because I've no idea what happened after leaving The Bell – I must've been spiked as I didn't even drink much - nowhere near enough to lose my mind, anyway…'

Her voice trailed off at the sound of footsteps descending the stairs, and Masud's heart sank at the prospect that Ronnie – Tilly's new love interest – would appear at any moment. An awkward few seconds passed as they awaited his appearance, which failed to materialise. Swinging her head impatiently around the doorway, Tilly encouraged the loitering presence into the kitchen.

'We're in here!', she called brazenly, and Masud was surprised by her newly confident bearing, her tentative nature switching suddenly to one of raw self-assertion. He busied himself as best he could with the careful pouring of coffee as footsteps approached, and he heard Ronnie's voice uttering a hushed and slightly strained, 'Shall we go, then?' as he entered the kitchen. Deciding it would be wiser to address the awkwardness head on, Masud turned to face Ronnie.

'Morning!' he chirped, perhaps a little too enthusiastically. 'Going anywhere fun?' A transparent attempt at glossing over a sticky situation, maybe, but he was aware that even the slightest hint of evasion on his part could be misinterpreted as suspect, and he wasn't about to risk that to give Ronnie an easy ride.

'Morning. W-we're just heading into town to get some food, I think', Ronnie stuttered, hands in pockets, floppy black hair falling over cavernous jet eyes: the picture of gawkiness, Masud observed, feeling a rush of sympathy for him. It was only the second time they'd met but he hadn't come across quite as gauche on their first meeting. Masud noted that Ronnie was poles apart from Tilly's previous boyfriend, who had been all pigeon-chested and testosterone-fuelled. He sensed poor rebound Ronnie would soon be on the scrap heap.

'That's the ticket' Masud replied, turning back to sugar his coffee, satisfied with his ice-breaking skills.

'You up to much?' Ronnie piped up, his voice a little more relaxed, as he began to edge towards the door, Tilly following serenely behind him.

'Sweet FA! As the cool cats say', Masud replied playfully, eliciting stilted laughter from them both as he carried his coffee to the kitchen table. He'd always felt most at ease playing the clown, even if others weren't particularly entertained. What with all those grey areas, why not splash some colour where possible?

'Enjoy!' laughed Tilly, smiling warmly at him as they stepped out of the front door. He sensed a genuine gratitude from her, presumably for his valiant attempt at smoothing things over, and savoured the sentiment; it was such moments that made life worthwhile.

'Cheers folks!' Masud shouted after them, a fleeting sense of relief washing over him as the door slammed and he was alone again.

But he remained far from reassured. Walking back into the kitchen, coffee in hand, he began to pace up and down. Although things had gone as well as he could have hoped for, and Tilly had appeared soothed by his honesty, he still felt uncomfortably in the dark, as if his home were privy to skeletons in a closet somewhere. Possessed by an insatiable curiosity, he found himself striding upstairs towards her bedroom, eager to discover something – anything – about the girl he had lived with for a year but knew almost nothing about. Never before had he felt compelled to snoop around his tenants' rooms, but something told him this was the only way he might ever come close to understanding the events of the previous night.

Her door was already ajar, and pushing it open, he was surprised by the degree of chaos he was met with: clothes strewn haphazardly across the floor, over the unmade bed and chair, a pool of red wine on the desk with an empty glass lying next to it and a distinctly musty smell lingering in the semi-darkness. Quite the opposite of the bright, ordered space he'd caught glimpses of on previous occasions. Looking instinctively towards the bed in the centre of the room, privy to a wealth of intimate secrets, he discerned a dog-eared notebook underneath a pile of books stacked haphazardly on the floor next to her bedside table. Of course she'd keep a diary, he thought, suddenly conscious of what he'd been seeking. Dislodging it carefully from beneath the incongruous stack of mind body spirit style hardbacks, The Art of Happiness by the Dalai Lama resting smugly at the top, he flicked through the pages, clocked some sprawling handwriting, and whisked it voraciously into his bedroom. Perching on his bed, feeling – quite possibly – more dissociated from himself than ever before, he opened the diary randomly at an entry from the previous week.

April 13th, 2015

Strange times – feel as if I'm sinking, barely able to keep my head above water. Had to cancel most popular yoga class on Monday mornings (probably a blessing) as my insomnia has reached epic proportions, and some nights I'm not sleeping at all. Have never experienced such deep unrest – impossible to settle, focus, enjoy the moment – as if my existence has dwindled to basic survival. But somehow I'm still swanning around teaching yoga, preaching the joys of inner peace and wisdom, despite the car crash my life has become. It's just one bloody fraudulent mess! I of all people should know that gorging on inordinate amounts of kale salad, taking regular saunas and sitting in the lotus position a few hours a day have zero impact on spiritual wellbeing if your weekends are spent in various states of loveless debauchery and your 'lover' is an emotional deadweight with an unshakeable hold over you. How did this happen? I've always been so balanced – people have pointedly commented on my stable disposition ever since I can remember, and probably still would (little do they know!)But when I compare myself to Masud, so eternally consistent in his habits and moods, I realise how frenzied a soul I've become. It's as if he's an emotional dial, the consistency of his nature gauging my wellbeing. If all is balanced in my life, I can happily sit in the lounge with him watching mindless TV, making light-hearted chitchat about the ins and outs of a day. But when I'm out of balance, he becomes repellent, the regularity of his being and his unwavering cheerfulness mocking my instability. Perhaps part of me sees him as a father figure, whose 'good example' I'm both respectful of and resistant to? One thing's for sure, though: his nurturing ways (cooked dinners, bike tweakings, general practical support) not only highlight my own inconsistencies, but make a blatant mockery of Ronnie's inattentiveness!

The root of the problem is that I'm fucking a liar - he drew me in with his gypsy charm and sweet nothings, just when I wanted to be swept off my feet, to believe in romance, two people making the world a better place – not an intolerable one, as it had been with Ben; Ben who refused to believe in magic, spontaneity or mystery – only cold, hard logic. But I couldn't drop the hope that he was something more than a charlatan, even when his beguiling black eyes proved to be windows to a dark heart; his spirituality another pretty lie. And every time we exchange words, bodies, fluids, I'm travelling further away from myself, my aspirations, authenticity itself. Starting to think I have a death wish...

Masud slammed the diary shut, catching his breath. Could these really be the thoughts of the poised and salubrious young woman he'd been living with for a year? She so ethereal and softly spoken, so hell bent on leading a healthy, balanced life that she'd emphatically refuse anything over one glass of wine on the odd occasion that they ate together. How had he been so oblivious to this secret life of debauchery? In all fairness, her fresh, youthful looks and obsession with pickled vegetables – the kitchen had begun to resemble a laboratory of multi-coloured jars– would be enough to throw most mere mortals off scent. As for Ronnie and his 'gypsy charm' – love is blind. He reckoned he wouldn't be alone in finding him about as threatening as a teddy bear.

Then there were her thoughts on him, heart-warming and soul-destroying in equal measure. Reading such raw, unfiltered commentary on his character had caused a stirring sensation to awaken in his gut, reminiscent of that which he'd felt as a teenager on overhearing a conversation about him between his mother and sister, which had gone something like:

'...You know what your dad's always said about Masud – he'll plod through life, no extreme highs or lows, no lofty ambitions, but he'll certainly make a good shoulder to cry on'.

Samiya, his younger sister, whom he had offended in some petty squabble, agreed reluctantly between sobs with her mum's consoling words, while Masud stood in the corridor, the insidiousness of what had been said creeping over him like a dark cloud moving with slow certainty towards his dismal future. But his dad had had a point, although he was loathe to admit it. He had always played it safe, stuck to a solid routine, never gone beyond his means or lost himself on the wings of fancy – not because he didn't have it in him to venture off the beaten track. Quite the contrary. He just knew that if he did, his instinct for escapism being what it was, he'd likely never return.

And so it was that friends and family gravitated towards him during crises, sensing a mysterious well of empathy within him, and he had vicariously experienced the repercussions of their foolhardy choices, but from a safe distance. Not that he'd remained completely detached from any personal entanglements. He'd been married for a few years once, and things had started off well, until she began to burrow her way into the delicate fabric of his life, her moods bulldozing over the peace and stability he held so dear. The solution was a no-brainer for him – a firm nod towards the door and back to his solitary comfort zone. A tenant for no strings companionship and a bit of extra help paying the mortgage had struck him as a less complicated alternative, although in light of recent events, he wasn't as convinced by this theory.

He felt compelled to tell Tilly that he was also a fraud, that everyone was a fraud in their own way. He used others to compensate for the emotional void of his own solitary existence, defensive as he was about safeguarding his independence, as she maintained the illusion of inner peace whilst secretly falling apart over some gawky low life. Something about life being a stage upon which we were all players sprang to mind – sitting in a stuffy classroom in Birmingham around 30 years ago, for the most part a disaffected sixteen year old, this idea had appealed to his teenage angst and identity struggles. If Shakespeare had penned it, it had to be true – life was just one big farce, which meant that the popular kids were just the best actors and that his stage persona could do with a bit of tweaking. Being a third generation Iranian with secular ideals had lent him a nebulous sense of self, so these were possibly the most consoling words he was ever taught at school.

Glancing at his bedsheets, scrunched up and blood stained, privy to some unknown action to which they were both oblivious, he felt moved by the mystery of this bizarre occurrence – a fascination rose within him. Tilly's unconscious had taken over, and by some inexplicable twist of fate, they had become entwined. Could this mean that something deep within her had wanted to be with him? Didn't they say that women go for their fathers, as men go for their mothers? And if she saw him as a father figure…her description of him as 'repellent' was grating, but couldn't the extremity of the word be linked to some latent feelings she harboured for him?

Returning the diary safely to its home under the musty pile of books at Tilly's bedside, Masud considered the possibility that he was sleepwalking through life, oblivious to the layers of primal meanings slumbering beneath the world of appearances. All he knew in that moment was that she would need a good, hearty dinner when she got home, so he set to work peeling potatoes.

It must have been around 9pm when she arrived home. He'd left the living room door ajar, so he could catch her before she rushed upstairs, as she had a tendency to do – especially when she was unbalanced, as he now knew.

'There's a plate on the side for you if you're hungry ', he called out. 'I cooked up a storm of a roast dinner earlier!'

She swung her head round the door, smiling wearily at him. There was definite apprehension in her body language now - no sign of the confident facade she'd displayed earlier.

'Sounds good - I was about to get a takeaway, but one of your roasts sounds much more tempting.'

There was no doubt she took well to being nurtured, unlike himself, who shied away from gifts of any sort. Knowing full well that she wouldn't be in 'mindless' TV-watching mode, he'd hoped the offering of food might lure her into some dialogue for a while.

'Go and help yourself', he laughed, bathing in the sentiment of rescuing her.

She sat on the sofa across from him, eating distractedly from the tray on her lap. The TV was blaring out its usual white noise, and despite his awareness of her contempt for it, he tuned in and out at his own discretion, finding it preferable to the deafening sound of silence.

'How can these people be so deluded as to think they have a talent?' she asked him, eying the TV incredulously, as if a UFO had just landed in its place.

'Lots of deluded people out there, I'm afraid, Tilly…'

Hearing his voice, paternal and world-weary, he was reminded of his assigned typecast as responsible father figure, and felt an insurmountable void between them.

'True', she replied, staring through the TV, as if into some distant, hypnotic realm that lay beyond it.

The stark realisation that they remained worlds apart drove him back to the reassuring presence of her diary, which he hoped would soon provide further insight into the mysterious events of the previous night.

'I'm off to bed now, anyway – enough brain-rot for me tonight', he said, a conscious effort to rally against the label of 'repellent landlord with rotten taste in TV programmes' to which he'd been assigned.

'Good idea – my bed's calling too', she agreed abstractedly, placing her dinner tray on the table and yawning her way past him, denying him a chance to actively prove his indifference to the banal nonsense she'd been staring through for the past twenty minutes or so.

'Delicious dinner, by the way', she added, some animation returning briefly to her voice.

'Just what I needed', she continued, turning briefly to acknowledge him.

Another look of unwavering gratitude - perhaps a hint of intrigue too. Had her unconscious journey into his bed roused the same curiosity in her as it had in him?

'Glad to be of service', he shouted after her, as she disappeared into the corridor, and up the stairs, her footsteps tired and lacklustre.

'Good night!', he cried through the half-open door, seeking a sense of security that continued to evade him. He imagined her reply, soft and soothing, beyond the steady hum of the TV.

Lying in his bed, sheets still unchanged and bloody, her scent lingering on the pillows, he realised that, perhaps for the first time in his life, he was unwilling to let grey areas remain grey. Everything about her had become, overnight, impossibly intriguing: the sound of her footsteps ascending the stairs, the soft, ambient music seeping through his wall, and most of all, her secret pains and struggles, of which she might at that moment be documenting.

Hearing the front door slam hours later, as he drifted off, he imagined her cycling on some wayward mission into the night, the accessibility of her diary rousing hope in him. Tomorrow morning might unravel more of the puzzle in which he had become embroiled.

It was habitual for him to wake at 6am, thanks to his job as a landscape gardener, which had had him on early starts for years. Leaping out of bed, roused by the prospect of more stupefying revelations, he headed downstairs to check if Tilly's bike was in its usual place. Reassured by its absence, he rushed back upstairs into her bedroom, the same musty odour permeating the darkness, and spotted her diary immediately on top of the unmade bed. Grabbing it voraciously, he flicked it open to the last entry and seated himself on her bed. As his eyes adjusted to the darkness, he dove into her thoughts with the same vigour as a deep-sea diver embarking on uncharted waters.

This has to be the closest to crazy that I've ever been – as if I've split in two, Jekyll and Hyde style, and am switching erratically between these opposing selves. A couple of nights ago, I was cycling to my yoga class, frayed and tired after Ronnie'd revealed he'd slept with another girl whilst I was away on training last month (he hadn't remembered any of it, apparently – just waking up next to her...reckons he was spiked at a house party...who am I kidding?!) Coming days after my discovery that he'd been lying about having a job at the Queen's Head for the past couple of months (what am I doing??!) I was starting to feel lost in some hyperreality, despairing of the part of me that was allowing this farce to continue. Running late for my lesson, I was cycling like a mad woman along the pavement, attempted to swerve around a bin, hitting it instead, and was catapulted into the main road, heaving with rush-hour traffic. Miraculously, the stream of approaching traffic had halted at the traffic lights around 30 meters from where I lay shell-shocked in the road. People rushed over from the pavement to help, and I felt strangely detached from the situation, as if I were floating in a dream. My right shin had two deep cuts where the pedal had dug into it, but I felt nothing and jumped back on my bike. Nodding as sanely as possible at the concerned strangers, I continued on my way feeling the fragility of existence like never before; all I could do was keep pedalling frantically into the soothing light of the full moon, the only truth I knew in that moment.

Heady from this torrent of revelations, Masud paused for a moment to resurface from the murky waters of her psyche. This was the stuff of melodrama! How could anyone get so embroiled in such a sordid world of secrets and lies? When he'd asked about her limp, she'd fed him a totally credible story about tripping up a stair in her yoga studio – tell the same story enough times and it becomes real, he thought. As for Ronnie – the mind boggled. How could she tolerate such abject immaturity and stupidity? Glancing at the pile of self-help books at her bedside, the Dalai Lama's enlightened grin fighting desperately through the gloomy room, a pang of desolation washed over him. He'd entered her world, immersing himself in its intricate tapestry, and it was anything but the colourful place he'd once imagined it to be. Yet all he felt to do was uncover its intricacies, delving deeper into her psyche.

Taught my Vinyasa Flow class with increased vigour that night, despite an emerging pain deep in my right thigh – I was alive, for fuck's sake – alive! Ronnie's response to my accident was typically dismissive: 'Almost died? Couldn't we all say that every time we cross a road and are inches away from oncoming traffic? The fact is that you didn't die, right?' Of course he wouldn't concede to playing any part in my wooziness, which he would have done implicitly by acknowledging the existential tightrope I was navigating. It was all part of our little game that he 'unwittingly' inflicted damage upon me and I shrugged it off 'obliviously'. To admit that I was falling apart was a huge diversion from the rules, but the rules – let alone the game – were starting to lose their appeal.

Masud was consumed by her words, falling down inside them like a tunnel. This was hypnotic stuff, and he was hooked on voyeurism. Ronnie had to be the most unthreatening sociopath he'd ever met, and he was sure he'd met a few in his time. She'd have to wise up to the most effective strategy in the book for dealing with those parasitic types – ignoring them. As for Tilly, how readily he'd accepted her at face value, seeing nothing more than a wholesome yoga teacher uncompromisingly dedicated to her practice. But weren't singular dimensions easier to compute? Never mind a dual self, her diary was fast succeeding in transforming her into a multi-faceted Picasso painting, opening him up to the unprecedented dimensions of her character, and for a brief moment, he questioned his ability to be with these new-found forms - payback for opening Pandora's Box? Thankfully, in keeping with his treasured Shakespearean philosophy, he consoled himself with the knowledge that his acting skills had always been impeccable, no matter what snow storms he might be experiencing internally.

A couple of nights ago, a crescendo was finally reached, my two selves colliding in a mysterious showdown. Ronnie and I went dancing with some friends, and I was feeling a breakthrough coming on, as if I were on the brink of new horizons. Since the night of the party something had shifted in me – a sudden awakening to the lunacy of my ways – and I felt as if I were hurtling uncontrollably towards some inevitable truth. I was drinking moderately, but seemed to be getting strangely high. My memory of the last part of the night is pretty hazy, but I have vague recollections of us lying fully clothed on my bed, a vibe of mutual disdain in the air. Next thing I know, I awake to a strange sensation, as if my mind is a vacuum, disconnected to the past, the future, all memory in fact. I open my eyes to an unfamiliar space, sunlight pouring through the cracks in an oak wood blind, and wonder if I'm dreaming. Looking down I see that I'm half naked and bleeding on the bedsheets. This can't be real, I think - I hope. Looking frantically around the room, the slow, painful realisation that I'm in Masud's room, Masud's bed, washes over me. My knickers lay on the floor at the side of the bed exposing a brazenly soaked sanitary towel. How the fuck did I get here? Was I raped? Did I cause a scene? Running into my room, I'm confronted by Ronnie's watchful eyes, scanning me coldly. 'Where have you been?' he asks, but I'm sure he knows more than I do. I lay down next to him, still half naked, and he tells me he's a firm believer in the force of the unconscious (as he'd said after revealing he'd 'unconsciously' cheated on me) and that he thinks he's 'bad' for me (a powerfully sadistic feat to drive your lover unconsciously out of bed). I laugh hysterically, get up, throw some clothes on and head downstairs to confront Masud, attempting composure despite still feeling completely out of it. Reassured by his relaxed manner and steady eye contact, my instinct tells me nothing happened between us, as my unscathed vagina had also pretty much confirmed. And for the first time in our short relationship, maybe Ronnie had a point – that it was my other, better self that led me to Masud for the sake of my sanity; it's just a question of how to be with each other now. Can we really maintain a semblance of normality after such a surreal occurrence?

Sitting motionless on the bed, submerged in the depths of her troubled psyche, her diary resting open on his lap, he felt his pounding heart driving him down, deep down into the primal waters of creation. Then a sound cutting through the heartbeat, a harsh overhead light piercing his retinae, her face looking down at him, bemused and at sea. Squinting up at her, he found that he was speechless; two figures floating in space, whose worlds had finally collided.

46

HINTERLAND

Lying awake in the small hours, Mark reflected on his recent bout of insomnia. Had the border that separated sleep from wakefulness become so blurred it was harder to cross? Was he sleepwalking through life?

His weak bladder was partly to blame. Only forty-six years old and already he was obliged to make at least three nightly trips to the toilet. The hours that followed had become vain attempts to empty his mind of futile thoughts, fluctuating between his audacious youth, the precursor to his current threadbare existence, and all of the possible ways – implausible as they seemed - that he might transcend his present day reality. So much lost in that fog; friends, business ventures, Norah and a twenty year old daughter, both of whom he heard from sporadically via hand-written letters across the Atlantic.

The obvious solution for a better night's sleep would be to cut back on his four-pack of real ales and subsequent whisky chaser – an inconceivable venture. He'd rather be a part-time insomniac with a photographic memory of every aspect of his woodchip ceiling than eliminate the main source of pleasure from his life. At least in those moments of mild intoxication he could find bittersweet solace in his old records, even his guitar on a good day, both of which had the ability to transport him to otherwise neglected realms of his soul.

***

Clara was exhausted by the day's frenetic activities. All she wanted was to curl up in the king sized bed in the musty spare room James had so kindly offered her, and be with herself. She sometimes wished life would slow down, despite being hooked on the adrenaline of travelling through time zones on a whim, visiting friends in far-flung corners of the globe, followed by more adventures on her home turf with friends old and new. But it was a rich life, despite the chaos, and she was never lonely, nor could she envisage ever being so. Nearly there now, she sighed, relieved at the sight of the intersection at the bottom of the main road to James's house, a landmark she'd come to equate with proximity to peace and refuge from the social whirl she resided in.

'Please see that her hair hangs long, if it rolls and flows all down her breast'… Dylan's lyrics resounded in Mark's head after an evening spent strumming them on his guitar. Nostalgic and wistful, they appealed to his romantic – or was it masochistic - streak, prompting thoughts of Norah and his golden days in Texas. Long, flame hued nights spent jamming under the stars, drunk on whisky and the energy of youth and music, Norah singing along beside him with fire in her eyes. He still imagined them all as they were then, in their prime, unwilling to visualise the cruel effects of gravity on those lusty faces. It was enough catching involuntary glimpses of his aging self, sagging in the most inconvenient places. Being a recluse was surely one way of preserving his dignity.

Soothed by the repetitive loop of the lyrics in his head and the fuzzy warmth of the whisky chaser, sleep took him surreptitiously under its wing, where he came face-to-face with Norah. Always young Norah in his dreams - the only version of her he had known intimately. She stood expectantly at the door of their apartment in Texas, wild eyes, holding their baby daughter. She'd decided to give him another chance, and he knew he would honour it this time, felt joy flooding in from a desolate place. Vague knocking sounds persisted somewhere in the distance but he was determined not to be distracted. As her nose brushed his cheek and moved seductively towards his mouth, making her usual 'stealthy' attempt to monitor his breath for alcohol, he understood that this feeling was beyond his normal range of experience - too good.

Painfully and inevitably, the warmth of Norah's breath transformed into the cold air of his small dark bedroom. But the knocking continued. Sitting up, he waited for a final confirmation that he wasn't dreaming, registered more thumping sounds and stumbled down the dark stairway. Must be around 4am, he reckoned curiously. He opened the door to a young woman, raven haired and bleary eyed, who greeted him with a look of relieved gratitude.

'So sorry to wake you but I really had no choice – only gone and locked myself out for the second night in a row but nobody's in to help me this time – thought I was in for a night on the streets!'

Her cheeks were flushed and her eyes, though bleary, were bright with warmth and sociability. Her voice rang in his ears, shrill like birdsong.

'Clara', she continued, reaching out to shake his hand. 'Just moved in with the boys next door, only a temporary thing – would you mind if I passed through your house so I can climb in through the back window?'

'Mark', he replied, ushering her through the door with a sweeping arm gesture, unable to think of anything more to say. Her grace only illuminated his torpor, how socially inept he'd become. He'd barely closed the front door before she'd weaved her way through the corridor and into the living room, a song bird with inbuilt navigational skills. On reaching the back door she spun deftly around to face him and he caught a whiff of alcohol fused with musk-scented perfume.

'Good night, Mark, and lovely to meet you – so sorry to have woken you at this ungodly hour.'

Her voice dropped to a whisper, she was apologetic but distant, embroiled in the dramas of youth.

'Not a problem – just don't go making a habit of it, eh'.

A failed attempt at wryness, he lamented, since her cheeks flushed a deeper shade of red in the kitchen's harsh strip light. 'Not that you would, of course', he added quickly, winking at her in jest.

'Promise I won't – I'll even wear a key around my neck for extra security if you like?', she joked awkwardly, edging out of the door, looking for an escape route, a quiet place to collect her thoughts. Her head was still whirling with the day's events and she'd drunk far too much to attempt to stick around and understand this man's strange humour.

'So long as I get a cut of your fortune when you start a trend', he replied, knowing it was a terrible comeback, and that he probably sounded like an ingratiating old pervert, but relieved not to have lost his voice completely.

Within seconds of switching on the outside light, he watched her leap gracefully over the fence, as if obstacles didn't exist in her world.

'Drop round for a cuppa some time', came a loud whisper from behind the fence and although he hadn't seen her face, he thought he noted a sincerity in her voice.

'Will do', he whispered back, closing the door, switching off the kitchen light and standing in darkness at the window. What must she have thought of him? A strange apparition in tatty blue pyjamas, no doubt, jowl and paunch overriding the mop of greying curls and marine blue eyes women had once considered striking. Unable to remember the last time anyone had invited him over for tea, he was temporarily jolted from his habitual emotional stasis. As his eyes adjusted to the hazy moonlight of the small hours, he watched dumbfounded as the girl sprung effortlessly up onto next door's window sill, formidably feline, and performed what he would have deemed to be an impossible task; with the powers of grace, youth and audacity she slid easefully through her friend's miniscule conservatory window, gone in a flash. Alone again, her scent still tickling his nostrils, he remembered what it was to be an opportunist.

Lying on her unmade bed, clutter spilling into every corner of the room, Clara relished this rare moment of solitude. The sterility of Mark's house had made her feel uncomfortable; tidy by her mum's standards, sparse by her own. The only splash of colour she'd observed as she'd sped guiltily through his living room was a small photo of a young girl, unframed and faded, propped haphazardly up on one side of the mantelpiece – his daughter, she guessed. But where were the relics, the objects that spoke of a full life? Could it ever be a choice to live like that? All she knew was that it would be impossible for her to exist in such a dead space, just as it was near impossible for her to sleep, despite her weariness, when life held so many possibilities.

Clara closed her eyes and began to process the day's events; picnicking in Castle Park, sipping cold lager at the graffiti festival, introducing the pale London man to her curious friends and walking him back to the train station in the late afternoon, sensing the possibility for romance between them sinking as fast as the setting sun. He had seemed confused about himself; perhaps she'd never see him again. But they had met, fused and departed from one another – magic how these opportunities for connection came and went. Then a text from an old flame, impeccably timed as she waved off the London man, watching the train curl gracefully out of the depot, a perfect emblem for beginnings and ends. Soothed by the bounty of life, its constant window of opportunities, her thoughts began to calm. Drifting off, distant sounds of sighing washed over her tired mind, subliminal as shifting sands.

Lying on the living room sofa, smoking a cigarette, Mark let out a long, deep sigh. He was tired yet roused as he reflected on his dream about Norah; how it had been a precursor to Clara's mysterious appearance at his door. Clara's exuberance had forced him to observe the sparseness of his existence. But still he felt strangely comforted by her visit, revelling in the surge of dopamine it had produced - a reminder of the exhilaration that social interaction could bring. The ceaseless humming of the electrical currents, usually a source of conflict to him, adopted a hopeful tone - hope, until now, a forgotten word - and sleep greeted him once more.

***

Finding himself in his back yard again, he knew what he had to do. She was waiting for him on the other side of the fence, tapping her fingers against the wood with the impatience of youth. The apprehension he felt as he prepared to leap into her territory was secondary to his excitement at being given another chance to follow her, a beacon of light penetrating his foggy existence. Surprised by his agility, he bounded over the fence with the litheness of a twelve year old, powered by a hunger for the zest she promised. She was already skirting the windowsill when he landed in the yard, enabling him to admire another of her effortless leaps into the unknown, Alice down the rabbit hole. This time, though, nothing was out of his reach. Springing onto the windowsill with the same nimble-bodied lightness as before and diving through the tiny conservatory window, he found himself bathing in a hot spring in his prime.

They were all gathered in their usual spot at the Rio Grande Gorge, merry after a skinful of beer and a day spent lounging in the Texas sun's unrelenting rays. Mark bathed naked in one of the many hot springs that resided at the bottom of the gorge, discussing his latest brainchild, the Green Energy Project with Neil, the other six dipping in and out of the conversation at their leisure.

'It had to be a hit, what with the new wave of hippies in New Mexico desperate to save the planet.'

Neil, also naked and recumbent in the spring, listened enthusiastically to his friend while juggling empty beer bottles. 'I gotta say, man – you've tapped right into a niche there. That federal grant you got's enough to turn the whole of Santa Fe into a goddamn jungle!'

The others cheered and howled, their voices echoing cartoon-like amongst the gorge's ruins. Grabbing his naked body from all angles, they hauled him out of the spring, launching him recklessly into the air. Relaxing into their firm grasps, he felt no distinction between himself and the infinite blue sky that engulfed his vision; solidarity, purpose and endless summer days – the bliss of starry-eyed youth!

'There's a lot of work to be done, don't get me wrong', Mark continued, dizzy from the bumps after being dropped back into the spring, 'but that's where the volunteers come in - green-fingered eco-warriors with a passion for getting native, edible plants back into the atmosphere. Something for lost souls out there to connect with too - great for their mental health. Combine all that with some solar power innovation and we'll be flying!'

Peggy, the sultry brunette who had joined them a few days before, looked at him hungrily, the type of woman for whom high ideals were an aphrodisiac. He knew he could possess her but she might expect more, as women often did, and he was attempting to patch things up with Norah now she was pregnant with his child. It had been going to happen sooner or later, the increased frequency of their reckless trysts flirting dangerously with probability. Besides, Norah was his girl; the one who wrenched his gut, despite her efforts to deprive him of the social whirl she knew was his life blood. He was still learning to channel his appetites.

Cracking open another beer, he gazed abstractedly at the mirage that emanated from the springs and sand banks ahead of them. In amongst the haze, he caught sight of a female silhouette on the river bank who beckoned him to her. At first glance he froze with ambivalence, convinced it was Norah, intent on dragging him away with her ceaseless demands. Once he'd placed it as Clara, he sprung to his feet, splashing frantically through multiple springs to reach her. Just as he came close enough to distinguish her features, huge dark eyes, impatient and eager, she dived into the river swimming rapidly towards Mexico. Once again, he knew he must follow.

Smoothly, subliminally they traversed the border, her head disappearing occasionally behind a wave, but never long enough to rouse fear in him. It was her forte to perform the seemingly impossible with insouciance, so he found his faith in her was unwavering. Remaining distinctly out of his reach, she was nonetheless a source of constant comfort to him, gliding over the waves as she glided through life, so he felt that wherever she led him he would gladly follow. On reaching the shore, she wasted no time, looking briefly behind her to check his progress – still around 100 metres behind – before running towards a glistening white cabin, a stark, angular structure sandwiched between an infinite stretch of yellow sand and blue sky. Three remote figures appeared to be waving to him from the veranda, a couple with clip boards, the other holding a briefcase, and he suddenly realised where he was meant to be - the meeting with his potential sponsors from the Forest Alliance. He was naked, but didn't care. All he felt was an uncompromising urge to shine for them, to win them over to his cause for the greater good.

Leaping up the cabin's wooden steps and gliding round the banister, he initiated firm handshakes with the three men awaiting him on the veranda.

'Delighted to finally meet you all', he proffered, with an impeccable sharpness of manner.

'Please, go on through', bellowed the figure with the briefcase, a tall, broad shouldered man with a ruddy complexion and affable blue eyes. The other two, both dressed casually in jeans and green polo neck shirts with Forest Alliance logos, stepped deferentially aside, the taller one ushering him into the cabin with an inclusive smile and welcoming arm gesture. Mark's nakedness and lack of physical aids did nothing to deter his confidence as he entered the small, shady room containing a long rectangular table with six chairs, and took a seat at the head of the table. The three men placed themselves evenly around the table and the man with the clip board addressed him encouragingly:

'Thank you for coming, Mark. All I'd like to say at this point is that we've already heard good things about you and would like to hear more. So, please...' His bold Texan voice hung in the air, eager to be crowned with Mark's vision.

'God knows there are unsavoury amounts of young people bumming around without a purpose today, just as there is an infinite amount of dead space in Santa Fe screaming out to be made energy efficient - green and lush at the very least'. Mark's words came urgently and vitally, rising from a well of undiluted conviction within him and something else, intangible but present, which spurred him to be the best he could be. He saw the men nodding in agreement, deferential and expectant, like hungry seals awaiting their next feed.

'No one could plausibly say we environmentalists are still on the 'lunatic fringe' now, could they? The smallest of the men, a slimline, dark haired figure hunched attentively over his clipboard, let out a hearty, concurring laugh whilst continuing to nod his head in agreement.

'The oil crisis proved to us all that oil consumption in the US is destroying the environment and crippling our economy. The government knows we are in deep shit - they practically forced this grant into our hands, told us to get a plan together quick sharp. So we secured the space, gathered together a large group of volunteers and realised there was potential to take things to the next level by bringing solar power into the mix – this is where you kind gentlemen come into the equation, with your worthy sponsorship.'

Mark felt himself glide through his speech with the same ease Clara had displayed as she'd glided over the waves, his conviction never faltering, those around him certain of his commitment to the cause. Glancing through the open door, suddenly mindful of Clara's absence, he saw her on the shore, mysterious as a distant vessel brimming with life-giving treasures. A sense of pride and conviction spurred him to jump in one last time as the larger man rose to say his piece.

'As I'm sure you gentleman know, we all need something to nurture - it's in our DNA. It figures, then, that if we are granted the resources required to nurture our planet, it will nurture us in return. This has to be the ultimate symbiotic alliance because we are all at stake – what worthier cause to fight for, what better sentiment to invest in?'

It was in the bag, Mark could see by the acquiescent glints in the men's eyes.

'We were already fans – you didn't have to say much to convince us of your ability to launch this project. Please accept this cheque for $100, 000 and go do your thing', the main man purred, his minions nodding in proud agreement.

'You won't regret this, folks', Mark said, accepting the token with unadulterated faith in its necessity. Shaking hands with each man in turn, still unified in his nakedness and sense of self, he thanked them for their donation and took his leave. Finding himself alone again, he knew he must rejoice with Clara, running impatiently down to the shore to tell her the news. Once there, he found nothing but the splashing waves and empty horizon.

***

He awoke to an unfamiliar feeling of acceptance. Fragments of the dream began to return to him, not wistfully as had often been the case when recalling dreams of Norah, but philosophically, like a memory of a long-lost loved one, where stoicism has replaced raw emotion. It was as if he'd been brought back to his senses by way of a mythical creature with a penchant for innovative trajectories. God knows he'd suffered for his sleepwalking, as had those he loved. But maybe it wasn't too late to experience that zest again, this time through less damaging means. How could he part with it now, having been so vividly reminded of how it had felt?

Clara stirred into wakefulness after a night of frantic dreams; parties, love interests and intrigue all featured among them, jagged imitations of her current reality. Even sleep was a strenuous activity these days, another adventure to navigate. Lying there, staring vacantly at the ceiling, no sound but the melancholy tones of a wind chime from the back yard, she was momentarily consumed by a vacuum of dead space; the potential meaninglessness of it all. Lurching out of bed, jolted by the horror of this anomalous thought, she remembered all the preparation she had to do for the house party that evening, clinging to the sense of purpose it brought. The secret, she thought, was never to stop.

The Youth Project Co-ordinator job Mark had seen advertised in yesterday's local paper, 'seeking confident, inspiring leader to support team of young environmentalists' now seemed more aligned with his capabilities. Placing himself at his computer, possessed with a focus he'd forgotten he was capable of, he completed the application form in under an hour, citing his influential position as an environmentalist in the States. Sealing and addressing the envelope, he walked out into the late summer morning, pausing briefly outside next door's front window. Clara's silhouette was perched at the back of the room, distant and unreachable, like the empty horizon he'd faced in his dream. It struck him then that tea had never really been an offer, and he continued on his way to the post office.

Sitting in her friends' front room, head full of plans for the party she was throwing that evening, Clara saw Mark's cumbersome physique hesitate outside the house. Wincing at the thought of him knocking, she had sensed a sadness in him that ran too deep for casual acquaintance. He cut a solitary figure, she thought, as he walked away – too solitary to invite to a party full of youngsters. Perhaps she'd invite her old flame though; she enjoyed flirting with life's possibilities.

FAST LANE

Ali headed towards the fast lane as she'd always done. It was her natural milieu, having long had the need for speed. Momentum was everything – to lose it was to lose that vital spark that powered creation. It was imperative not to slow down. Slowing down was the beginning of stopping and to stop was to surrender to mortality.

Striding past the slow and medium lanes, she nodded perfunctorily at the handful of regulars gossiping at the pool's edge. Life in the slower lanes had always struck her as frivolous and unfocused, triggering some deep-rooted belief that everything should serve a purpose. Yes - she was being unfairly judgemental. The fat, decrepit old man who lingered habitually at the shallow edge of the slow lane, barely swimming at all, obviously needed to be validated by as many young women as possible before he finally keeled over. Who was she to cast judgement if his main purpose in life was to exist under the illusion that he was God's gift to women? At least as a middle-aged woman she'd become invisible to that type of man. Anyhow, the slow lanes were for dreamers, if not drifters and decrepits. The world needed dreamers as much as it needed realists, she thought, adjusting her goggles firmly over her eyes and tying her hair into a tight bun before plunging into the shallow end of the fast lane. The challenge lay in bringing the dream to life.

Standing to attention, sharp eyes narrowed to a squint beneath her goggles, she waited intently for her break. Life had required these moments of intense focus in order that she'd got what she wanted from it: resisting the patriarchal narrative of marriage and children, challenging the complacent authority of know-it-all publishers and literary critics, were all choices which had meant keeping one eye firmly on the game. Now, perhaps more than ever, this skill seemed key to her survival. And there it was – her lucky break! She dived deftly into the opening, knowing how illusive they could be. Dreamers seldom caught these openings – reveries got the better of them. They missed boats. Now it was about staying in the game; sussing out the rhythms and idiosyncrasies of the competition as she might scrutinize a journal she hoped to be published in. Ali jerked her head round to see who was on her tail and was relieved to find a poised young woman engaged in an elegant crawl a few feet behind her. No threat there, she thought. Women respected boundaries in confined spaces. It was men you had to watch.

With this thought, she became aware of turbulent waters ahead. Hardly surprising that the balding middle-aged man in front of her had decided to slow down on a whim and have a leisurely splash around, oblivious to his environment. Some might say she'd tempted fate. She would cite hard empirical evidence acquired over the years. How many times had she been stuck behind one of these half-witted exhibitionists? Too many – that was certain. Which reminded her that a magazine still owed her for a short story they'd published months ago – she had sensed from the editor's facetious telephone manner that he was the sort of man who prided himself on being difficult. Case in point.

Slowing down and stretching her neck as far out of the water as possible, she shot the offender, who continued faffing complacently on his back, one of her death looks. He caught it, but carried on throwing his weight around as the elegant young woman behind her swanned past with three committed swimmers in her wake. The horror of invisibility pulsed through her. Keep up the pace, she told herself, dropping her head back down to the water and breaking into a crawl, so as to overtake the object of her irritation. At least you don't have to contend with that flailing idiot now.

Instead, unwelcome thoughts of her consultant flooded into her mind. She wrestled with them, as she wrestled with the compulsion to touch the intractable tumour that clung to her right thigh bone. How would she tell John? Telling him would only consolidate the depressing reality of her condition. At least their separate living arrangements meant she could bide her time.

Just keep moving and it'll be fine.

Another keen swimmer powered on ahead of her, gracefully combating any obstacle that interfered with her path. The fast lane made no concessions. Every man for himself – and a handful of women too - it was where she belonged: a progressive environment where momentum sustained ambition. Each mile-long session she swam generated a wave of heat in her, usually followed by another chapter of her sequel to Shout Louder, a satirical novel exploring the dark side of #metoo. Shout Louder had received international acclaim – and the obvious backlash from hard line feminists accusing her, much to her amusement, of being a 'masculinist'. A far cry from the 'strident feminist' she'd been labeled by one critic recently following a playful article she'd written on how to be a woman – what a scream to have hit the binaries! This alone made her feel like she'd made it.

Although she didn't care much for the 'isms', Ali took less offence at being described by one critic as an 'existentialist' - existentialism was an ideology she could better relate to. Here they all were, sculpting out their destinies in their respective lanes – actions and choices that would impact the course and rhythm of their lives. Idle chit-chat in the slower lanes might be soothing in the short-term, lending itself to procrastination as it did, but she had tended to view strangers in this context less as vessels of comfort and more as obstacles around which she must skillfully manoeuvre. She felt no need to make friends at this stage in her life – it was hard enough staying in touch with the handful that she had. That said, the stamp of anonymity she'd credited the fast lane with endorsing had begun to feel more like invisibility. Its dogged persistence struck her now as lacking humanity.

Her consultant was of a similar ilk – greeting her at his desk that morning, silver-stubbled jowl smacking of unchecked affluence, his gaze sank through her, as if he were contemplating how he'd like his steak cooked that evening. Such a nonchalant countenance had filled her with hope – whatever she had, it couldn't be life-threatening - until he began pulling ominous-sounding terminology out of his specialist hat. Words such as 'Non-Hodgkins Lymphoma' 'slow-moving', 'low-grade' rolled glibly off his tongue, his eyes still faraway. The lives and deaths of his patients appeared as inconsequential to him as the queen's latest hat. All she could possibly be to this man was an unfortunate statistic that brought him closer to his pay-packet.

Once he'd finished reeling off the technicalities of her diagnosis, his sunken grey eyes attempted momentarily to engage her.

'Do you have any questions?' he asked, his tone raising slightly in a vague suggestion of humanity.

'So I've got cancer?' she asked, gripped by her usual compulsion for definition.

'Yes', he replied, attempting solemnity.

'How long have I got?' she demanded, impatient with his obscure medical terminology.

'It's treatable and the most common slow-moving strain of lymphomas. People with this type of cancer can go on leading normal lives for years in fact', he said, leaning back defensively in his chair.

Much as she wished she could be convinced by his reassurances, she struggled to find integrity in his bearing. Like the flailing egoist, oblivious to the feelings of others as he splashed complacently in his power, this man was not invested in seeing her.

'Right', she replied, a note of scepticism lingering in her voice. All she knew in that moment was she couldn't remain a second longer in that stuffy room.

'There'll be more questions – undoubtedly', she continued, rising from her chair and eying him intently so that he promptly averted his gaze.

'I just need some processing time', she concluded.

'Perfectly natural – we'll discuss treatment options and pending blood test results at your appointment next week. Expect a call within the next day or two confirming the details', walked out of the room.

Holed up in her car in the hospital car park, she scanned the pamphlet, attempting to channel an emerging sense of panic into concentrated stoicism. Her gaze fixed on the sentence 'stage 1 or 2 can offer good prognosis though later stages may be highly treatable as well'. Hadn't he used the word 'treatable' to describe her condition? So he *was* withholding vital information from her. This was surely justification enough for why she hadn't trusted him and his shield of medical jargon – as if his sprawling paunch and spurious eye contact hadn't been enough of a giveaway of his need for an easy life. It never ceased to amaze her how few people were able to get to the heart of things – especially matters of life and death. Doctors, it seemed, were no exception.

***

Ali paused for a moment at the shallow end, battling a breathlessness she was unaccustomed to experiencing. She'd always harboured an impatience for illness in others, having managed to push through minor ailments herself with will power alone. So long as the mind was strong and vital anything was possible, she thought, admiring one of the regulars - a dark-skinned Adonis - as he glided past her in full impeccable butterfly stroke. It was this kind of brilliance she'd do well to tune into now. But the sight of an old couple eying her anxiously from the edge of the medium lane filled her with dread. Then a concerned voice to her right drew her attention back to the space she inhabited.

'Um...excuse me – sorry. Don't mean to be rude, but have you considered trying one of the slower lanes?' enquired the elegant swimmer who'd sailed past her earlier, her approach so tentative it was impossible to take offence. Ali was nonetheless taken aback.

'Honestly I can't say I have', she replied curtly. 'I've always swum in this lane and have no intention of switching now', she concluded, satisfied with the dispassionate authority conveyed in her voice.

'Only a suggestion', the woman said, raising her hands defensively. 'It's just you seemed to be struggling a little', she continued.

'Well thanks for your concern – it's been a long day – but I'm perfectly fine', said Ali, plunging back into motion, galvanized by this unexpected challenge. Gaining momentum with her crawl again, she considered the implications of the woman's enquiry. Was it made in a spirit of irritation masquerading as concern, as the sceptic in her was inclined to believe, or was it in fact genuine? The old couple in the middle lane were still watching her as she made her way back towards the shallow end. They appeared to be anticipating a crisis, the woman's foreboding expression triggering childhood memories of her mother when tensions ran high.

The fast lane and all of its connotations would have been inconceivable to her mother, although she'd lived her life at a faster pace than she'd wanted to. Conforming to the bourgeois spirit of the fifties – marriage, children, piety and hardship – had meant her ego had never found its full expression. Her literary talents and adolescent fantasy of becoming a poet had been displaced by a philandering husband and two demanding daughters. Fortunately her spirit wasn't completely crushed due to her life-long fellowship with God, but the 'daily drudgery' she'd often described her adult life as being led Ali to believe that her earthly soul had remained largely unfulfilled, in a state of limbo.

There had been an introspective quality to her mum that wasn't conducive to motherhood – when Ali recalled her, waiting at the school gate, cooking, cleaning, her gaze was beyond the tasks at hand, beyond her and her sisters, as if she were elsewhere. A weary fragility had enveloped her, so that Ali wondered whether taking the path of least resistance had taken the most extreme toll on her vitality. It was this compromised state she'd resided in that Ali feared most. Everything in her fought against the concerned looks from the middle lane; the urge to compromise her desire to plunge headfirst for a softer, more subdued activity; the urge to surrender to a lacklustre life, as her mother had.

Despite remaining faithful to her crawl, Ali felt as if she were a piece of driftwood at the mercy of an unforgiving current; then came the sensation of her days being numbered in a sudden wave of panic. Fifty-two years old and she'd never felt a day over thirty. Now it seemed she was hurtling towards invisibility, the determined spirit that had always kept her out of trouble suddenly redundant. Never had she felt her destiny to be so out of her hands. Her heart raged against her chest as the gravity of her condition struck – grasping at the pool's edge for support, she found herself lost in space, alone with death moving in on her; alone while others cruised on, oblivious. Her vision became narrow and distorted as she began to hyperventilate, feeling them all to be vessels on a conveyor belt from which she would soon be taken. Then a round, pink face sprang into her line of vision, innocuous grey eyes twinkling warmly at her, soft firm hands grabbing her shoulders. It was the old woman from the concerned looking couple.

'It's okay, love – you're just having a funny turn', she said in a mothering tone.

Mothering. Motherly. But not her mother. The softness of the woman's touch was redolent of her own mother. In her ruffled state, nothing could have been more soothing as she suffered her first panic attack. Definitely the first consolation she'd received from the realms of the middle lane. Being out of control was what other people did – not her. She must be dreaming. Too bad the fast lane wasn't for dreamers!

'It's okay – thank you', Ali said, removing the woman's grip on her shoulders and attempting to breathe deeply. 'I forgot to put my lenses on this morning – just came over a bit dizzy but I'm fine now'.

'Could've fooled me', said the woman, eying her protectively. 'Looks as if you've seen a ghost!'

'You're not far off, there', Ali laughed, making her way slowly towards the steps. 'Thanks for your help', she said, nodding as steadily as possible at the woman, who continued to eye her intently as she hauled herself up the steps. But the nostalgia that had gripped her for maternal warmth didn't move her to continue the conversation. All she felt in that moment was an unsettling combination of attraction and repulsion towards the woman, followed by a compulsion to strip off the wet costume that clung to her body like crippling shame.

***

'Welcome back, Ms McShane', said the consultant, addressing her with the same glazed look.

'Thanks, Mr Williams. I wish I could say it was my pleasure but circumstances wouldn't appear to permit', Ali replied.

'Circumstances are not ideal, although the type of lymphoma you have has proved highly treatable', said the consultant, his pink jowl wobbling defensively. 'There are a number of effective treatments available, which we can discuss today'.

'All well and good, Mr Williams, but before we discuss treatment options I'd like to raise what seem to be a couple of pertinent issues with you', Ali said, re-crossing her legs and elongating her spine in preparation for what she had to say. Her days in the fast-lane might be numbered but she had no intention of exiting the driver's seat any time soon.

'First off, I noticed in the guide book you gave me last week that this condition is potentially incurable – quite a significant piece of information to withhold on our first meeting don't you think?', she asked coolly, attempting to hold his gaze before it sunk through her again.

The consultant's small blue eyes darted evasively to the notes on his desk, which he picked up and shuffled into a neat pile, before placing them gently back down and resuming eye contact with his patient.

'We were still awaiting crucial results last week, Ms McShane, without which it would be impossible to determine the severity of your condition. A treatable condition – I do believe I used the term 'treatable' – is indeed distinct from a curable one as I assumed you'd understand.'

He took a slow inhalation of breath, as if preparing for turbulence that would require him to exit his position on autopilot.

'My point entirely, Mr Williams. So what you are suggesting is that my job as a patient is to read between the lines of my diagnoses? To view your indirect terminology as a puzzle in semantics that should be solved independently?'

Mr Williams' deadpan expression morphed into a smirk.

'Nothing of the sort, Ms McShane. However, as consultants delivering unfavourable news, we tend to avoid the head-on approach in the early stages, favouring a more delicate delivery of potential outlooks until all test results have been finalised.'

'I demand nothing more than to be spoken to directly at all times, Mr Williams – every eventuality revealed. I refuse to view my wellbeing as a riddle waiting to be solved – this is my life and I want to know where I stand.'

'Naturally, Ms McShane, and if you'd like me to adopt a more head-on approach, I'm happy to do so', the consultant deferred, his face reddening under the strain of unprecedented challenge.

'Your adaptability would be much appreciated', Mr Williams', she said, a mocking tone lingering in her voice.

Mr Williams nodded decisively at her, as if keen to move on from the subject of his professional delivery.

'Nevertheless', he announced, his voice straining for optimism. 'You'll be relieved to know that your recent test results indicate that your condition is stage 1.'

Ali looked quizzically at her consultant, her head tilting abruptly to the right, as she considered once again the integrity of the man in charge of her destiny.

'Funnily enough, the second issue I'd like to raise with you is regarding the stage of my lymphoma. Correct me if I'm wrong, but after conducting my own online research, it would seem it's impossible to diagnose stages without having a bone marrow scan to determine whether or not the cancer has spread to the bones – am I right?'

Mr Williams fiddled nervously with his gold wedding band. Shiny beads of sweat had begun to sprout on his brow.

'If the cancer was in your bone marrow, Ms McShane, you can rest assured the blood tests would have picked up on it', he asserted defensively.

'And that is a certainty, Mr Williams?'

'Indeed it is', said the consultant, his obsequious tone belying the trepidation that flickered in his eyes.

'Well you're the professional so I'll take your word for it', she replied, a hint of irony in her voice. She had already resolved to seek a second opinion. There would be no giving up the ghost just yet, although if that was her swansong she considered it a good satisfactory.

64

Ali approached the middle lane with philosophical intent. Her energy levels were low and it was necessary to preserve as much life force as possible to fight the disease. It was not a defeatist move, she told herself. Not regressive. She was simply attempting to adapt with grace to her condition. If she never had to confess to John that she was dying of a terminal illness - not just suffering from her annual turn of burn out - the world would be a brighter place. There was only so long she could continue to lead a double life of medical consultations and date nights, despite the horror she felt at revealing this creeping vulnerability. But surrender seemed to be the only way she could break free from the trappings of her fate.

Lowering herself into the water, she was struck by the disorderliness of the lane at close range. Clusters of mostly women, and a handful of stray men, swimming clumsily back and forth, oblivious to any lane etiquette as they gossiped voraciously, resulting in frequent near-collisions with divergent clusters. Here in a nutshell was everything she had spent her life trying to avoid. Just when she thought she'd escaped the distractions of idle chitchat, and was about to get her head down, her surrogate mother called out to her from the top of the steps.

'Coo coo m'love', chirped the jovial dialect.

'Oh hello!', said Ali, fighting her instinct to plunge into her usual anonymous abandon. Instead, she reached out her hand. 'Don't think we got round to formal introductions last time. I'm Ali'.

'Wendy, my love', said the old woman, clasping Ali's hand heartily. 'Joining us tortoises over here today, are we? Never thought I'd see the day the way you push yourself over there – can't be good for you, dear, over-exerting yourself like that.'

'I over-exert myself in most things I do', said Ali. '"Go hard or go home", I believe they say. Rather take the plunge than dip a toe in, if you know what I mean?'

'I know just what you mean, m'dear. My husband - the gentleman usually here with me - used to be like you. Always powering ahead over there on his own mission, no time to spare in the slow lanes. Then the poor love got lumbered with Parkinson's and had to slow down. Tis a cruel world sometimes, eh?'

'Sorry to hear that', said Ali, struck by a pang of guilt at her former dismissiveness of the couple. But Wendy's husband had been a fast-laner too. A man on a mission, before succumbing to the ambiguous fate of the middle lane.

'If it's any consolation, I've got cancer', said Ali impulsively, surprising herself with the candour of her revelation; how readily it rolled off the tongue. Must have been Wendy's soothing, matriarchal qualities that softened her edges. She held her gaze, which evolved quickly from friendly concern to knowing compassion.

'Honestly, m'dear, can't say I'm surprised. Even before your funny turn last week, John'd picked up there was something awry with you. Takes one to know one, so they say', she said, winking charitably at Ali.

'Well he was spot on there, although I was loathe to admit it', said Ali, glancing over at the fast lane, teeming with its regular competitors. She shuddered at the image of her ailing self, swimming against the tide. No wonder they'd been giving her strange looks!

'Is it a vicious sort?', the woman asked, pursing her lips together as if she were in pain.

'Depends what stage I'm at', said Ali. 'I've requested a bone marrow scan since my consultant appears to have such spurious knowledge of his speciality. From what I gather, it's at best curable, at worst managable'.

'Strong woman like you'll go on for years', the woman said confidently, her fierce, wise tone providing Ali with reassurance she hadn't realised she needed.

'I'd like to think so', said Ali, feeling suddenly overwhelmed with claustrophobia. As if switching to the middle-lane hadn't been enough of a seismic shift, without indulging in a heart-to-heart with her surrogate mother over an issue she'd not even found the words to raise with her partner.

'Best get moving while I still can, then!' she continued, spurred into action by the sight of the fat old man in the slow lane leering at her. Didn't he know she was dead meat?

'That's right, dear – best get to it then', the woman called out as she broke into a crawl.

Gliding past a few dawdling middle-laners, Ali felt affirmed by the buoyancy of Wendy's assertions. Yes - she had always been robust and proactive, and was comforted by the old woman's perception of these attributes in her. Had part of her been resisting such nurturing qualities ever since she'd begun to resist her mother? Receiving accolades for her books and publications had – she believed – surmounted any other self-affirming needs she might have. Dry, intellectual musings and critiques of her work had served to validate – and occasionally invalidate - her existence. But perhaps there were some needs that remained unaddressed, lurking in the shadows of the middle lane.

Ahead of her were a couple of young women swimming side by side, talking in slow, reflective tones, their eyes on no fixed point. Once again she was forced to slow down, but felt less frustration in doing so now. Directionlessness struck her as less infuriating than entitlement, but somehow more difficult to be with. She recalled her mother's dreamy expression, its inherent fatalism – her needs could never be met in such a climate. Then a dark haired man came powering towards her from the deep end, oblivious both to her and the clockwise etiquette so clearly advocated. Something in him had resisted the fast lane, as something in the two nattering women had resisted the slow lane. The comfort of sitting on the fence, perhaps - or the bother of choosing between one distinct path and another. Had her mother's passive approach to life irked her in much the same way that the medium lane did? Had she herself ever really broken free from this realm or was the dark-haired man her alter ego – swimming against the tide of mediocrity, claiming to be something more?

Ali reduced her pace as she approached the shallow end. She had come to the middle lane to slow down, after all, even if everything in her rallied against this. But its undefined parameters made her feel like she was in purgatory. Perhaps she was – her mum had always threatened she'd end up there unless she changed her dissolute ways, which had consisted largely of remaining unmarried and child free. They were, after all, punitively selfish – how could a young, healthy woman like herself choose not to bring children into the world? The idea that birthing children onto an already overpopulated planet might actually be construed as more selfish had been impossible for her to understand.

Selfishness, in her mother's eyes, had constituted any behaviour that didn't ultimately require self-sacrifice through service to others. Stemming from this self-abandonment arose a series of meltdowns, many of which Ali could recall as sharply as if they were yesterday: her mother raging tearfully over the stove, tipped over the edge by an unsuccessful omelette; her mother engaged in frantically poor attempts to conceal scratches on her cheeks that her father had given her; her mother bringing out breakfast in the mornings with puffy eyes and a strained smile. No wonder she'd resolved to put her own needs first.

If her mum had died in limbo, dreams unfulfilled, Ali reasoned it was her duty to rise up from her maternal ashes like a phoenix and doggedly pursue the gift she'd inherited from her. But being her happy ending had meant leading an autonomous existence free from the shackles of family. She'd resisted biological urges on the grounds that she'd rather aspire to do one thing well than aim for some unrealistic 'do it all, have it all' notion of feminism. Some might say she'd resisted her femininity for success in the fast lane – maybe she had. Living was reactionary. A partner on the sidelines was the limit of her romantic capabilities, but John had accepted this life choice admirably. An artist himself, he'd understood the necessity of having, at the very least, a room of one's own.

The dark haired man was racing towards her again, still on the wrong side of the lane. He glanced intransigently at her, willing her out of his line of vision. Momentarily overcome by a sense of her own frailty, she capitulated. Resistance, she felt, would have cost her too much. There was little doubt that this had been her mother's reaction to men – easier to put her attitude aside and submit than to put up a fight, despite her enduring robustness. But Ali's feelings of frailty were proving a revelation to her: to worry she might lose her footing climbing steps, or to question whether she had the energy to rise from a chair in one exerted push were predicaments she'd never previously conceived of. This decline in robustness had created a fear that took increasing precedence over her decisions – the possibility that the obstinate dark haired man might cause her further harm by bulldozing headlong into her had outweighed any inclination to put him in his rightful place. She found herself seeking warmth over justice; a different kind of self-preservation.

Ali experienced the soft eye contact and polite smiles of the middle lane as more conducive to her wellbeing than the unreceptive fast-lane politics she'd once thrived on - the relief of having nobody on her tail; nobody to answer to. Leaning against the wall of the shallow end, she saw Wendy wading towards her from her faithful spot at the far left.

'Call me nosy but you got me all curious, now', said the old woman, a concerned look in her eye. 'I only hope you got someone to take care of you through all this?'

'If you want to know whether I'm married, the answer is no', said Ali, smiling knowingly at Wendy. 'I do have a partner but we live separately and having no children has meant we've never had to make serious decisions about commitment', she continued, hesitating for a moment.

The old woman smiled bewilderedly at her, eyes squinting keenly, as if all of her energy was invested in understanding Ali's words.

'I suppose we've both clung to our independence', she concluded, immediately questioning her use of the word 'cling' - surely it was incongruous within the context of independence, in the same way that persisting with the fast lane had been when she was running on empty. So much energy spent keeping people at arm's length.

The old woman continued to look bemusedly at Ali, as if mirroring her own thoughts.

'But you've told him what's going on with you?' she asked tentatively.

'Not yet – not sure I'm ready for the reality check, if that makes sense?', Ali replied, aware of the absurdity of her argument.

'Well you're made of stronger stuff than I am – that's for sure', said the old woman, beaming at her with a look of baffled adulation.

'Hmm. So strong I can't even tell the man I love I've got cancer?' retorted Ali.

'You're only trying to protect him, dear', asserted the old woman, her voice faithful in its resolve.

'Not sure it's him I'm trying to protect', said Ali, challenging her newfound ally's committed bias.

'Course it is. I've met folk like you before – all hard shells an' soft centers.'

Wendy's blatant attempt to read her triggered a sudden urge in Ali to escape back to the fast lane, away from Wendy's prying eyes. There had been some relief in talking openly with a stranger, but it seemed the old woman was attempting to get close to her and this she couldn't handle. Her mindset should remain as neutral as possible now, without being diluted with sentimentality. She felt herself scant and evasive next to the openhearted robustness of Wendy. She knew she had to tell John – she would go to him as soon as she was dressed.

'Thanks for listening, Wendy – you seem to know me better than I know myself', Ali said, making her way towards the steps, wondering again if she would make it up them without sliding through the cracks.

'Go and tell him, love', said the old woman, winking at her.

***

Ali approached the slow lane under no illusions. The beads of sweat on her consultant's brow had spoken for themselves – he had known, at least feared, that her condition was terminal and that he had failed to implement the correct measures for diagnosis from the start. The scan she requested had revealed what she'd suspected – that the cancer was in her bones; that large tumors surrounded her lungs and groin, and that she was on borrowed time. Too little time to sue for vindication's sake – she'd grilled the poor man enough as it was. Barely time to surrender to her own fate.

'Never thought the day would come when I'd see you this end', said the fat old man, lingering in his usual spot towards the left side of the shallow end.

'I never thought it would either', said Ali, making her way warily down the steps, gravity weighing heavily on her dwindling frame.

'Suppose it would be rude of me to ask what inspired such unprecedented change?', said the man, his voice deliberate and pensive. Whether he was oblivious to her stark weight loss and unmistakable frailty or just being polite she couldn't decide.

'It might well be considered rude, since we are total strangers, but it's probably a bit late in the day for me to be precious about such things', said Ali drily. Again she felt the urge to plunge into a vigorous crawl, sidestepping the rawness of their interaction - then the pain of that impossibility.

'The grim reaper's on my tail so circumstance dictates', she continued. 'This is where I belong now.'

'Well I'm Chris', said the man, reaching out his hand benevolently. 'Shame our meeting is a result of such unfortunate circumstances but honestly speaking, I don't think you'd have given me the time of day otherwise so at least I get something out of your misfortune', he added, winking unapologetically at her.

Ali found Chris's offbeat humour preferable to any maudlin expression of sympathy.

'You're probably right there, Chris', she laughed. 'Watching life go by has never been my strong point – nothing personal of course... I was just doing my thing and chasing time over there – caught up with me in the end though'.

'It's a different pace of life this end', a black haired, olive skinned woman chimed in as she reposed with her head against the poolside, arms stretched out to the sides. 'We come here to reduce the tempo whereas you Speedy Gonzales over there want to amp it up', she asserted, eying Ali with brazen curiosity.

'If only you'd told me that before I'd have been over here in a shot', said Ali wryly, as the two pairs of eyes surveyed her disconcertingly. Their stationary presences seemed to be holding a mirror up to her, forcing her to look at herself.

'Jokes aside, we're probably more similar than you think', the woman continued, her voice clear and decisive, with a Devonshire twang. Ali put her at a maximum of 35 years old.

'Women with responsibilities - perfectionists in our own rights. Only difference is that I cut myself some well deserved slack when I can'.

'Good for you', said Ali, sensing integrity in the woman's conviction, all the while feeling increasingly harassed – even exposed. She had always managed to avoid this kind of personal scrutiny, her deftness of mind and body having served as buffers against it. But resistance seemed more futile than ever in her current state, and this woman was clearly not the sort to be deterred by theoretical diversions, let alone terminal cancer patients.

'Sometimes you've got to learn the hard way', said Ali, smiling wearily at her antagonist, inwardly questioning why she'd never been able to cut herself some slack. She thought back to her mother's dreamy disposition, how those moments when she'd seemed closest to herself she'd also seemed lost to the world. Had she always feared losing herself in this way? Not fulfilling her earthly purpose? Whatever the reason, it seemed mothers always got the blame - even if the most plausible explanation lay in her own avoidance of the pain of self-knowledge.

'Probably seems strange to you, but we come here to relax, have a natter, watch the world go by', the dark haired woman continued, her cattish green eyes pinning Ali against the wall and stripping her bare.

If the middle lane had been purgatory, Ali wondered if she might now be in hell – a place where people made unrestrained judgements with scant consideration for others. Or maybe it was heaven, where freedom of expression prevailed, for better or worse, in the name of truth and piety? Either way, she couldn't have felt any more removed from her natural habitat.

'Not strange at all - just not how I rolled in my fast lane days', said Ali, scrapping her heaven and hell theories and wondering instead if she was about to be subjected to an earthly crucifixion. Had these people no reverence for the dying or were they emblems of death's absurdity?

'Aha! Just as I thought,' guffawed Chris from the sidelines, still listening keenly to their conversation as his legs thrashed back and forth in the water.

Despite finding the woman abrasive, Ali was drawn to her ease of being. She imagined her at school as the archetypal rebel nobody claimed to like but everyone was secretly in awe of. Her expression was freewheeling and uninhibited – qualities that struck Ali as starkly opposing her bookishness, which lent a stilted manner to her communication.

'Are you a mother?' the woman asked.

'No', said Ali.

'Explains all the excess energy you had', said the girl.

Her use of the past tense was not lost on Ali, stinging her temporarily.

'I've got three kids and love 'em to bits but need some me time now and then, otherwise I'd lose the plot.'

'Good for you', replied Ali, unsuccessfully attempting a neutral tone. The woman seemed to be suggesting she was mad, which made for an unsettling exchange.

'Being childless might have played a part in my energy levels, although mothers can be prolific achievers on nervous energy alone', she continued, eying her tormentor quizzically. She seemed to have held onto a fierce and vital aspect of her character, despite being a mother of three. There she was in full alpha command of the driver's seat, preaching her philosophy in the slow lane.

'Sure they can but I'd rather not become a nervous wreck if I can help it. I give myself a break when I can – something's gotta give, and it's not gonna be my health or sanity', she said, a look of devastating candour in her eye.

Ali considered the woman's words, wondering what it was that had given in her life, and her mother's introspective gaze flashed back to her once again. As a child, she'd viewed her as being at her worst in those quiet, unresponsive moments, but the likelihood was she'd been at her best, alone and at peace with herself. Those moments had no doubt stopped her going mad amidst the chaos of domesticity, as Ali's need for speed had energised her introspectiveness, propelling her to experience as much of life as possible, which in turn kept her sane. Two sides of the same coin, it seemed each had sought solace in what the other had too much of.

'Enough about me, anyway. What about you? Are you happy with your lot?' asked the woman.

'Now there's a question I'd never have been asked in the fast lane', said Ali.

'Is that why you spent so much time over there?' the woman retorted.

The night before, John had compared her to a star in a galaxy with lots of space around it. He said he'd accepted years ago that he'd never really know her but loved her all the same. She'd found his declaration strangely maudlin – John had never been one for displays of sentimentality – but it resonated with her all the same. Despite her drive for success, she'd been too afraid of her own light to see it reflected in anyone else for too long; she'd kept people at arm's length and hidden behind words as her mother had hidden behind God. But John loved her like a lonely star.

'I've been asking myself the same question', she said, glancing again at the fast lane where people powered on, driven and focused, heads down. She'd spent her life attempting to be the force her mother could have been; keeping up momentum, finding a voice and forging a path for herself in what remained a man's world. She'd pushed herself to the limits, to avoid becoming her and, paradoxically, to avoid some lurking fear of not becoming her. Sometimes there was no winning. Reaching for the tumour on her groin, she felt it embodying her many pains and joys: the cost of living was higher for some than others.

'And?' demanded the woman, impatiently.

'And - shall we start swimming?' said Ali.

'Swimming? Thought you'd get it by now. This lane's not for swimming, love', said the woman, recumbent in her power.

Printed in Poland
by Amazon Fulfillment
Poland Sp. z o.o., Wrocław

54806239R00047